THE LEATHER POUCH

Part 1: The Land of Kings

Elaine DeRegnier

Bookman Marketing
Martinsville, Indiana

ISBN: 1-932301-50-X

THE LEATHER POUCH
INTRODUCTION

This novel is fiction and therefore told in English. The Frenchman, Simon de Regnier 's family stories, re-told through generations, have two common themes--survival and immigration to America. Simon, called "Monty," cites the words of Frenchman, Jean Sartre. In telling stories, "I self-motivate myself to discover it."

CHAPTER 1: THE DEPARTURE

On a dank, smoggy day, in 1858, Monty stood alone at the ship's cold rail in fog-filled solitude and wondered, what led to this horrible predicament that surrounds him?

He stood, one among hundreds of ill-clad strangers, lonely and sad. Immigrants were fleeing oppression, but he, merely seeking opportunity. Did he belong on this ship? Looking down at the ship's oak planks and thinking his feet no longer touched French soil, the anticipation of the new world, dulled for the moment. Forlorn and ensnared in woeful conditions, he questioned, how did this begin? Thinking back, the day Max missed work was a beginning of his new world interest; when his father, Jody, had said, "Max, I missed you. Were you ill?"

"Nein, felt bad. Got vord my brother, Otto, his wife, and four children emigrate to America. Is last of family. I hear bad stories about ships transporting immigrants."

"I am sure they will write you from America. Where are they from?" Asked Monty's mother, Adrianne.

"Westphalia. Brother say Germans from Hanover, Oldenburg and Saxony go and many craftsmen and farmers. He wrote ship dock at New York. Is in middle of ocean by now."

"Do not worry, Lafayette crossed the ocean many times." Jody tried reassuring him as he scratched his mass of curly black hair; black hair outlined by a hairline that formed a peak and receded at each side of his forehead. A peak that accentuated his lean and well-cut features. Though small boned, yet he towered over Adrianne. He was a man who could not sit without crossing his legs; did not matter which leg as long as one leg was resting over the other.

"Yah, but could I not have had early notice? Could have invited me? Not that I vould. Otto be so far away. In new vold."

"Uncle Maxie, what is the new word?" Asked Monty, in his manner of habitual childhood curiosity. He had his father's ears, small and laid back; ears that heard and questioned everything. One could see a glint of humor in his direct and intense dark brown eyes. Typical of the Regniers, his head was large and sculptured in classic form and feature. Definitely, handsome at any angle.

"Not vord. New vorld, Monty. Land different than ours."

"What kind of land?"

"America. I tell you someday."

"Another helping of lamb stew?" Adrianne pushed the tureen towards Max.

"Tell us now." Begged Eddy, a handsome clone of Monty, except for the black, curly hair of his dad, and blue eyes of his mother.

"Quit pestering Max. Eat your supper." Adrianne changed the news from Max's family. "Did you see where Tocqueville's book is being translated into English? I am glad he has been elected to the Chamber of Deputies." Peeved that Adrianne changed the subject, Max replied with the bizarre, "Yah, and Frederic Chopin lives with novelist, George Sand. He vant a woman, he no pick trouser-ladden mistress."

"I read the Americans captured the Seminole Indian leader, Osceloa," said Jody, "and that he died in prison from malaria."

"Tribe dat never surrender? Retreat into swamps?"

"Yes, smart move on their part."

"Jody, I am going to dress Monty and Teddy in their best, and have Daguerreotypes taken to give the folks at Christmas. I stopped to inquire at the studio and it costs dearly, but would be worth it."

"Dress boys in finery. I pay."

"Oh, I didn't mean ..."

"Never you mind. Dat's settled. Vant picture of boys and self. Vant picture myself mit doz little gamins. Send one to Otto and ask him send picture of his family. Jody, vhat you tink of earthquake in Martinque?"

"It is hard to imagine Fort Royal was practically destroyed."

"I am clearing the table. Move yourselves to the rockers. I want to begin Volupte, the book Irene sent on Charles Sainte-Beuve's love affair with Victor Hugo's wife."

"You and your lady friends do not have enough gossip? You have to read scandal?"

"May I remind you, your sister sent it to me. Angela, Irene, and your mother have read it."

"Jody, better vatch her. Be donning trousers like George Sand or American, Charlotte Parkhurst."

Adrianne indignantly cleared the table and pretended not to be listening while she washed dishes. Her blue eyes set wide apart, gave Adrianne an appearance of being attentive and curious. Her mouth added charm, especially when she smiled. She was lean, a muscular well-built woman, who appeared to have extra long arms because of her exaggerated gestures when she spoke. She was stately and poised in composure.

"Who was Parkhurst?" Jody asked.

"Customer, dat been in Paris told me people in Cafe Voltaire discuss her. She like benefits of being male. Had no trouble passing as man. Smoked cigars, drank, and chewed tobacco. Consider her one of best stage drivers."

"One of these days, you will have to join me at Le Rubis tavern."

"Nien." Max was hostile to socializing, while Jody and Adrianne Regnier were an outgoing, optimistic couple interested in people and France's changing government. Revolutions had changed the society of eastern and central Europe. Rural social revolutions echoed the one launched sixty years earlier in France. Liberal principles and fear of popular revolt went hand-in-hand in imposing changes upon the landlords in Europe. Feudal society had come to an end all over Europe.

"Since Victor Cousin reformed our educational system, I am amazed at Monty's progress in school; and Eddy is showing improvement." Said Adrianne.

"Yes, noticed Monty is advancing quite fast."

"I asked him to review his subjects. What had he learned in art? He mentioned Corot and Millet and told me about a group of landscape painters near the forest of Fontainebleau, called the Barbizon school."

"Have not heard of it."

"Neither, have I. He said a Jean-Louis Meissonier painted a lot of Napoleon's battles."

"I have heard about his work. What has he learned in history?"

"He spoke about Algerians. The Zwawa tribe, members of our infantry corps; the Zouaves we replaced with our soldiers. Told of German Amanas, who migrated to America; and said the farmers in America outnumber city people, six to one. He said William Frederick IV, King of Prussia, has gone mad; and told me about David Livingston, a Scottish missionary, exploring Africa and tracing its rivers. I could tell his interest centered on America."

"What in America captures his interest?"

"The frontier. Told me the Oregon Trail was 3200 km long; and spoke of a frontiersman called Kit Carson. Also, mentioned a Matthew Perry, commander of America's Navy African Squadron, who is suppressing the slave trade."

"What about Victor Hugo? The champion of republican ideals. Are they teaching anything about him?"

"Now, you know he is too young to be studying politics."

"I do not expect him to be reading, Nikolai Gogal's, Dead Souls, that grotesque lampoon on Russian feudalism. I suppose French history is censored under this regime. How is he doing in literature?"

"Read Joseph Marie Sue's, Les Mysteres de Paris and Le Jif Errant."

"What? He is reading about the Parisian underworld and expressions of socialist sympathies? He does not need to be exposed to those ideas."

"Please, do not start trouble with the school. Monty said he had read The Pathfinder, and Charles Dicken's, Nicholas Nickleby, Old Curiosity Shop and The Christmas Carol. Adrianne shifted the conversation and asked, "Since I can not travel this late in pregnancy, shall we invite Max for the holidays?"

"Yes. I think it would be welcomed."

Typhus had taken Max's wife, and he had since quit celebrating holidays. He was a recluse bachelor until he hired Jody to work in his cabinet shop. Max knew townspeople only as customers, and made his store purchases quickly and without neighborly talk. When he built his house, he had gruffly refused anyone's help. For an old man, Max had perfect Prussian posture. His shaven, Aryan features were distracted by yellowing, poor teeth. He wore old, worn workclothes that were neat and clean. He smelled of sawdust and had rough, stained, boney hands. Max was taking his lunchbreak of goat cheese and sweet white bordeaux, when Jody extended his invitation.

"Vat? Spend Christmas mit you?"

"Adrianne is fixing magret of duck served with a foie-gras-enriched sauce, clafoutis, poached pears and souffleed potatoes for Reveillon. She is making her favorite recipe for tripe, a la mode de Caen for Christmas dinner, and for dessert, lemon mousse with prunes. She will be very disappointed if you refuse."

"You no go home dis Christmas?"

"No. Adrianne's in the fifth month. The trip would be risky."

"I tink about it." The invitation left Max shocked and unprepared with an answer.

"You do that. In the meantime, we will be counting on you."

School had closed for the holidays and the boys frolicked in the falling snow. Max came striding down the street with a fir tree hoisted over his shoulder.

"Uncle Maxie. What have you got?" Shouted the boys and crowded around him.

"Christbaum. Boys open door for me."

"Welcome, Max. What are you doing with the tree?" Adrianne asked.

"Tis Christbaum. Decorate for holidays."

Jody asked, "Where did you find the tree?"

"Green-thumb. Plant in backyard. I cut for holiday. Effen Queen Victoria's husband, miss his Christbaum when he move to England, and now he decorate one in Windsor Castle. We, too, have one."

"Decorate? How do we decorate a Christbaum?" Asked Monty.

Eddy said, "I kept a dried mushroom from last spring. Can I put it on the tree?"

"Dot vod be fine. Your mother gather candles. We put candles on tree and Weihnachtsmann put gifts beneath." He was elated, to have given the family their first Christmas tree, and proudly arranged the tree's crushed branches in symmetrical fashion.

"Who is Weihnachtsmann?" Asked Eddy.

"Ach, dot be Christmas Man."

"He is like Pere Noel." Said Adrianne.

"There is story bout Christbaum."

"Tell us the story."

"We have read Hans Christian Anderson's story about The Fir Tree." Said Monty.

"Story different. Long ago in Middle Ages, peasants perform plays about Adam and Eve in church. Actors hung apples on branches and symbolize tree of good and evil. Then Church ban plays. People bring tree into homes and decorate mit roses and vafers which stood for Mary and Jesus. Adrianne, I vill be glad to come next week for Reveillon, Christmas, and Bonne Annee, and partake of delicious food."

"Tell us another story, Uncle Maxie." Whined Eddy.

"Here Max, help yourself to cheese, crackers, and wine. Rest and relax, after totting that tree through all this snow."

"Tell us a story." Eddy repeated, and scooted his footstool closer.

"Now boys, Max may not have any more stories."

Max was eager to hold the boys attention. "I am filled mit stories. Vant to hear about Yule Log? Goes back to time before Christ vas born."

"Tell us." Eddy sat on the his stool by Max's feet. Monty sat nearby.

"Once upon a time, people burned logs during vinter solstice to bring light, warmth, and hope during dark days of vinter. Light from log gave faith dat spring vould come and crops grow plentiful. Believe log's fire scare away evil demons and spirits, and give warmth to ghosts of ancestors. Scandinavians burned log in honor of Thor, their god of thunder. People believe it protect them from thunder and lightning. So they burn log short time during Christmas and save for later, vhen thunderstorms break out."

"In France, it was once thought burning yule logs helped the animals conceive." Said Jody.

"Dad, French people thought that? I do not believe it."

"They did. Would soak the log in water and give it to their cows to drink, and thinking there would be as many calves, goats, chickens and lambs, as there were sparks in the Yule log."

"Oh, dad, your stories are not as good as Uncle Maxie's."

Each day, more gifts appeared beneath the tree. Adrianne was resting in a rocker when Max came with more packages. "Max, you will spoil the boys with gifts."

"Nien, just spoil self."

On Christmas Eve, Max attended Mass with the family and returned to enjoy the Reveillon meal. The Christmas compensated for many he had missed. Bonne Annee brought a rebirth of himself. He bubbled with joyful excitement over the gifts he give. Max and Jody were relieved the holiday rush orders were completed. Jody asked, "Max, let us go to Le Rubis."

"We dressed for it?"

"We all come in work clothes. I will tell Adrianne and meet you out front."

"Let us join this group. I know the men at this table."

"Hello, Jody." Said Henri. The men scooted together to make seating room. Jody started, "I would like you men to meet Maximillion Casimir. Call him Max. This is Henri Etienne, Wilheim Louvois, next to him is Gustav Poussin, Jules Fleury, and Ivanovich Ruell. He goes by Ivan." Jody ordered two ales.

"Max, what do you do?" Asked Henri.

"Carpenter and cabinet-maker. Slow time. Decide to come here mit Jody."

"Same with my work. Slow after holidays." Said Wilheim.

"Yah, your shop is vhere?"

"West side of town. I have passed your shop and admired the cabinets sitting in the window."

"You, Gustav, are compagnon. A mason." Said Max, recognizing the significant gold earring in his right ear. Jody is compagnon."

"I run the livery on this side of town." Said Henri Etienne.

"My bookstore is just a few blocks from here." Said Jules Fleury.

"I am your mayor." Said Ivan Ruell.

"Ivan, what do you make of the disturbance in the northwest part of town?" Asked Jody.

"Widespread unemployment is creating a rise in violence and a new edge to radical movements everywhere. The commercial slump is starving our cities. Revolutions are going on all over Europe. The successful revolution in Vienna means the dislocation of all central Europe."

"Germans now free to revolt mit out fear of Austrian intervention. Italians turn on Austrian armies, Hungarians revolt in Budapest and Czechs in Prague."

"They want national independence, not constitutionalism." Said Henri.

"June days of the Paris uprising gave the Revolution a shove towards democracy, but failed, at the cost of many lives." Said Ivan.

"In the past, defection of our armed forces permitted successful revolution in Paris, but now such forces are available to our government. The battles of the June days were destined for defeat." Said Jules Fleury.

"We are lucky our so-called Citizen King, Louis-Philippe, abdicated. His support of us middle class citizens turned into repression." Said Ivan Ruell.

"Did he flee to England?" Asked Henri Etienne.

"Yes. Although Europe is plagued with internal revolutions, we can be grateful we have not had war for thirty-three years." Said Gustav Poussin.

"Gus, our sons are near conscription age. What do you think of Louis and Hortense de Beauharnais' son? Napoleon's nephew, now in power? I am skeptical. What can we expect?" Asked Jody.

"He certainly used the prestige of his Napoleon name to win the presidential election. Better we watch out for that fellow, Otto Bismarck. He has come into prominence since the June Revolution." Said Wilheim Louvois.

"Vell, dat was interesting. Glad you invite me."

"Stay for supper? We can continue our conversation. You know, Monty will soon be going off to join the compagnons." Monty heard his dad's comment. "No, dad. I do not want to join the compagnons, but Eddy is interested."

"Since when did you make that decision?" Asked Adrianne.

"When I found out Eddy wants to be a compagnon."

"Do you, Eddy?"

"I like working with my hands, carving and building things."

"What do you propose to do, Monty?" Monty had his answer ready; he had thought about it a long time. "I want to farm. I will work in the shop until Eddy returns as a compagnon. Then I will go to America."

"Go to America? I will not hear of it." Said Adrianne.

"Mom, it will not be right away."

"His dream, mom; he talks about it all the time." Said Eddy.

"He has not talked to me."

"He comes by it naturally, Adrianne. Dad is a farmer, the family has been farmers from way back. His leaving is not welcome, but he has a right to his choice in life." Said Jody, and thought about the leather pouch hidden under the tile.

"Vouldn't be going off to war."

Cynthia Louise was born in the spring, according to Hoyle. Jody explained to Max the family's traditional expression used at births. Max failed to see the humor associated with the idiom, and felt "liebling" or "prinzessin" more fitting. "She not have birth velcomed by reference to game book of rules." Max had brought the children books by British novelist, Captain Frederick Marrat. The Children of the New Forest for Cindy. The Mr. Midshipman and Masterman Ready for the boys.

France had another coup d'etat dissolving the Legislative Assembly; and Napoleon III declared himself emperor. His domestic policies fostered industry and the planning work of Baron Haussmann, transformed the face of Paris. The Industrial Revolution spread from England into the continent. England's railroad grew to over 5000 miles, and the iron-horse was the talk of the continent. Boatmen on French canals brought their families on board as crew to save money from competing railroads, and a distinct way of life grew from the canal folk. Railroad clocks imposed uniformity on commerce. The post made changes, and mail was delivered at a faster rate. Growth and building created a demand for compagnons.

A proud Jody had taken Eddy to Paris, where he passed the compagnon tests. Cynthia Louise and Andrianne bemoaned Eddy's absence. Jody added spare francs to the leather pouch as increased business kept Max, Monty, and himself busy in the shop. One day the post brought a letter with the news Jody's grandpere Luke had died.

"The horses are outside. Are you ready?" Jody asked.

"As soon as I get this bundle on my back." Said Adrianne. Jody mounted the horse with Adrianne behind him. Monty raised Cindy and placed her on the hired, second horse and mounted. The trip allowed Jody time to grieve, and as he dwelt on recollections, the monotonous gallup of horse-hooves beat out memory after memory. Living far away had its price. They arrived the day before the funeral.

"Did he suffer?" Asked Jody.

"No, he died in his sleep of a stroke." Said Angela.

After the funeral, Adrianne's parents, Hubert and Jeanne, stayed for the reunion. The families of David and Damon had not increased. Jody's Cindy, was the baby in the group. His nieces, Mary and Marie, were spoiling her with attention. The family knew Eddy joined the compagnons, but were stunned to hear Monty planned to go to America.

"We will never see you again." Moaned his sister, Angela.

"I think it is great. Going where land is available. Farming is the best work for any man." Said Damon, who was Irene's husband and helped farm the homestead.

"You need not urge him on." Said his younger sister, Irene.

"I have copies of Horace Greeley's, New York Tribune. Tells of a movement of High Germans from central and southern Germany who immigrated. Monty will be in good company." Said Jacque, who was Damon's brother, and owned the village bookstore.

"America had a two year cholera epidemic, but was checked by cold winter weather. Had a summer epidemic of yellow fever, and in New Orleans took 5000 lives." Said Hubert.

"Jacque, you have newspapers from America? What is happening over there?" Asked David, Angela's husband, who owned the tobacco store.

"It is amazing, all the happenings. Zachary Taylor died in office and Millard Fillmore became president, then Franklin Pierce. The Mexican War has ended. I saw in the New York Lantern, a cartoon character Americans call, Uncle Sam. A California gold rush is going on. Elisha Otis invented elevators and tall, cast iron buildings are being erected. A news service called the Associated Press was organized. A sewing machine was invented by Elias Howe. The Barnum Circus is exhibiting a midget, called Tom Thumb. Have something called chewing gum. It has replaced paraffin for chewing. Odd, because it was introduced by a despised enemy--General Antonio Lopes de Santa Anna, who massacred troops at the Alamo in Texas. Mexico exiled him and he entered the United States and brought a chunk of chicle, the sap of the Mexican sapodilalla tree, which he loved to chew. A local inventor, Thomas Adams decided to market it, since his son liked chewing it."

"I read Uncle Tom's Cabin. The book has created a national stir over slavery."

"Yes, Hubert, the book is sympathic to slaves. Slavery has split America into those for slavery and those against."

"Jacque tell us more." Monty asked.

"Japan was closed to foreigners, but America managed to opened relations. America has a process for making evaporated milk, patented by a Gail Borden. Monty, do you have a bookstore near you in Le Mans?"

"Yes. Jules Fleury has one."

"Ask for the New York Tribune. If he does not have it, he can order it." Jacque said, "When in the bookstore, I overheard women talking about the American woman, Amelia Bloomer, who speaks of women rights and wears baggy, black pants. Pants called, bloomers." Jeanne and her sisters giggled, and left with Adrianne and her mother to get away from the men's conversation. "Angela, have you heard anything about the dauphine?" Asked Irene.

"Yes, in the journal, L'Inflexible. Had a stroke of paralysis that crippled his limbs, but he recovered. Fasted and prayed, and became a monk. He wandered to Rome for an interview with Pope Pius IX. After that, he no longer wished to be restored to his inheritance."

"He no longer claims to be the dauphine?" Asked Irene.

"He is not denying it; just withdrew from the public."

Jeanne asked, "What did you think of the opening of the Crystal Palace Expo?"

"It was nice England declared the opening day a holiday."

"Irene, it was because of Queen Victoria's wedding anniversay." Jeanne added.

As Jody's family bid adieus for Le Mans, Jacque handed Monty two books--The Oregon Trail by Francis Parkman and Moby Dick by Herman Melville. Monty lingered with his farewells, emotionally flustered knowing he would be leaving and not seeing his family again.

Leaving a France where Napoleon III had improved sanitation and public utilities, that destroyed much of the medieval part of Paris. A Paris, now turned into a city of beautiful dramatic vistas with long avenues radiating from the Arc de Triomphe, and the Tuileries with rows of yews and clipped trees. A Paris with its roses, boxwoods and clipped lime trees in the sixty-three acre garden Andre Le Notre designed in 1664 to embody the image of a new France and ornament the Louvre. Paris was again, the City of Light, but Germany was the power in Europe.

The labors of shopwork, carving banisters, constructing frame-work, and sawing, did nothing to erase Monty's memory of her. Hammering did not shake her from his mind. In the evenings, he silently tried to read, but thoughts wondered aimlessly on her. He had said nothing about Millie. She, who had hair the color of coal and eyes that lifted his spirit into a blue sea of heavenly thoughts. Millie had peered into his soul and found him. The girl on the right side of the cancan chorus line, who smiled down at him from the stage. Their backstage meetings had been brief, filled with lust and passion. He knew only, that she was the youngest in the dance troupe and the oldest of nine children. Their talks were brief before she returned to the stage for another dance number. He had asked her to be his bride and travel to America. She preferred a man named Ulster, who said he would get her into the Bourgeois Follies. How could she leave with Ulster? Monty swore never again, to go to Le Regine. He wished her the worst. Yet, longed for her presence. In his despon-dency, he felt only an army experience would dim her memory.

While working in the shop, Monty asked, "Dad, did you say Eddy would be home soon? He has completed the Tour de France?"

"Yes. Finished early, as I did."

"I have changed my mind. When he returns, I am joining the army. Russia occupies Moldavia and Walachia; Turkey has declared war against Russia. We are bound to be pulled into the war."

Jody was shocked and angry. "Going to America. That is what you had planned. That is what you will do. You think about it. In the meantime, do not say a word of military talk to your mother."

Max was listening to the conversation and stopped his carving to say, "Vhat's matter mit you, Monty? You never go to America if you not go vhile young."

Eddy came home to the family's enthusiastical welcome. Jody

pondered over Monty's army plans, until the uncertainty overwhelmed him. He was moved to action and retrieved the leather pouch and American Speller from beneath the kitchen tile. "Monty, here. These are the savings, squeezed from their labors beginning with Lambert Andre, Peter Antoine, Joseph Mark and Bert Lucas. Passed down on their deathbeds to me. Savings meant for the first member of our family to immigrate. Take it, and start planning your voyage." Monty took the pouch of dreams. His dream of Millie, paled in comparison. "I will go to America."

"I want to go." Wailed Cindy.

"He does not need to leave so soon. Eddy just came home and we ....." Said Adrianne

"Yes, he does. Britain and France will soon be in war against Russia. Would you rather he go to war?"

"War? Oh, no, how can that be?"

"Talk at Le Rubis is that the diplomacy of Napoleon III is leaning that way. He will embroil us in this war. Eddy's safe, being a compagnon, he will be needed on the home front. Monty would be conscripted."

"Of course, I would rather he go to America, than war." She quickly went for some salacin to ease her headache. A remedy the French chemist, Frederich von Gerhardt, contrived from powder drawn from the bark of the willow tree and the extract of the meadow sweet plant.

Adrianne invited Max and was fixing a culinary delight for Monty, who would leave the next morning.

"Heard from Otto. Are vell, and plan to stay in New York. Monty, vhat is your route from here?"

"The coach goes to Laval, through Rennes and then St. Brieuc. I will buy passage on the first ship leaving for America. I may have a delay in booking passage. The Constitutionnel reported many immigrants were traveling from there."

"Here. Otto's address. I wrote you vould maybe look him up. In last letter, he say you buy cutaway coat. Take out those ballooning hoop-skirted ladies. Girls vorking in America called, vaitresses. Maybe you find nice, plump, healthy one, and marry her, nien?" Max asked.

"There are many railroads. Do you suppose you will be going on one of them or staying in New York City?" Asked Jody.

"Wish I could ride a railroad." Said Cindy.

"Will leave New York City and take a railroad to Chicago. I plan to stay there and save for a farm."

"Remember, vat Otto say bout "runners." Try to vindle from you, your money."

"I worry about yellow fever and cholera." Said Adrianne.

"Mother, those epidemics are over."

"I will sew the leather pouch into your undergarments. Bandits are robbing coachs." She applied more damp cloths to her forehead.

Jody said, "I would sure like to see those trotting horses and baseball, so popular over there."

"Monty, as new American, vill you know one thing. Who be president?"

"President Franklin Pierce," Monty answered with a grin.

Two passengers got off at Le Mans, as Monty stepped into the coach. A man remained, reading a book, who said he came from Chartres. Monty was filled with excitement and bittersweet feelings, as he viewed the passing countryside. He thought of Paris, and Peter Antoine, who was born back in 1682; and the old stories told of Peter and Paul's escapades into Paris. Parts of Paris had not changed. Only events had changed, not the Paris landmarks. Peter Antoine was called the family attester, because he had been a trouvere father. The first ancestor remembered as having passed his knowledge onto the next generation in the manner of northwestern medieval poets.

He had, as the story goes, been taken by his father, to the Marionette Theater at the Luxembourg Gardens, and on a tour of the Hotel Guenegaud, with its decor of hunting and nature themes designed by Le Mansart. Peter marveled at the collection of weapons, trophies, stuffed stag heads, antler chandeliers, inlaid gun stocks, cross bows, and the stairwell made of wrought-iron stags running along the balustrade. His father had pointed out the handcarved 10'4" high fruitwood clock made in Belgium with twenty-seven pounds of mercury in its pendulum. His father had sadly related the ironic fate of the Moliere House, where Moliere died in an armchair while acting in his own play, The Imaginary Invalid. The family still had Peter's books: Charles Perrault's, Contes de ma Mere l'Ole (Tales of Mother Goose), Daniel Defoe's Robinson Crusoe and Johathan Swift's Gulliver's Travels, and a few torn articles from the London Gazette, edited by Sir Richard Steele.

Clearer in Monty's mind were the talks of Peter and his friend, Paul, who owned a boucherie chevaline (horsemeat butchery). Talks about the Rye House Plot. The conspiracy to murder Charles II of England and his brother, Duke of York; where Lord William Russell and Algernon Sidney were tried and executed.

Talks on the tournament Henry II gave for his daughter's wedding, and had died on the square of the Queen's Pavilion near the church Eglise Saint-Paul from his jousting wounds. His tales about Charles V, The Wise, the king during the Hundred Years War with England, who built a vast library in the tower of the Louvre, which King Francis I, later added an enormous amount of works to the library and brought back the Mona Lisa from Italy.

The spoken accounts of trips to the Cafe Procope in Paris, with its crystal chandeliers, mirrors, and marble tables. The cafe founded by a Sicilian, Procopio dei Costelli, who served the exotic New World drink of cafe (coffee). The heavy curtains, barred windows, and deceptive, secretive haunts and affairs of the first Parisian cafes.

Buddies, Peter and Paul, had looked down along the Seine, seeing the Louvre on the Right Bank with its fishermen, and told about Philippe Auguste, who built a wall around Paris and the Louvre palace. Told how Charles V changed the fortress into a palace for his home and King Francis I, chose it as his court. Stories of the Cite Fleurie in south arrondissments, the oldest artists' colonies in Paris and of junk dealers and rag pickers on the northwest end of the eighteenth arrondissment. The descriptive tales told of the Rouvre forest and the twelfth and sixteenth arrondissments that bracketed Paris with dense woods. The story of the foolish duel of Madame de Polignac and Madame de Nesle, when the slightly wounded Nesle was carried off on a stretcher, Polignac yelled, "Let me at her. I'll eat her heart."

Monty had learned much about Paris history from these stories that spoke of the canals and adventuous barge travel. Stories that told of the Grand Chateau in Versailles, the residence of kings which had two smaller chateaux--the Grand Trianon and Petit Trianon; whose architect, Le Mansart, also built Les Invalides in Paris. How the gardens were done by Le Notre, who also created Les Tuileries--the playground of Paris. Learned of the Marais, a district that borders on the quartiers populavies of the Bastille, where the mansion Hotel de Sully lies in the third arrondissement. Heard how the marais (swamp), being uninhabitable until the thirteenth century, was changed when monastaries and convents braved its unpredictable waters to build. Spoke about the Notre Dame--the Soul of France.

As each farm passed from view, Monty remembered bits and pieces of Peter Antoine's war-torn life. There had been: the Third Dutch War, when the king invaded with help of British sea support;

. . . the Great Swamp Fight. King Philip's War in America, against Wampanog Indians;

. . . England's Glorious Revolution when King James II fled to France, and William and Mary accepted the Bill of Rights and established a constitutional monarchy;

. . . Monmouth Rebellion where Duke of Monmouth, a Protestant, opposed the Roman Catholic succession of his own uncle;

. . . Revocation of the Edict of Nantes, where over 250,000 Huguenots emigrated;

. . . the prince Savoy, who fought the Turks and freed Hungary;

. . . Wars of the Grand Alliance between France and England, Austria and the Netherlands;

. . .Great Northern War when King Charles XII of Sweden invaded Denmark and attacked Russia to be overcome by Russians under Peter the Great, who fled to Turks, who in turn defeated Russians;

. . . War of the Spanish Succession--the third European war, Louis XIV's attempt to increase French power;

. . . Queen Anne's War between England and France over possession of North America.

Monty thought of the many wars in Peter's lifetime; then whimsically, how he must have been a rogue to do all the Paris traveling. He married Magdeline Besaneon and in 1702, begat the next generation--Daniel Pierre.

The countryside was changing, and no longer resembled his home area. The temperature was cooler. He rummaged in his bundle for a sweater.

"Where are you headed?" Asked the male stranger.

"St. Brieuc."

"I get off at Rennes. I teach literature. My name is Frederick de Lodivier."

"I am Simon de Regnier. What are you reading?"

"A new book by Gustave Flaubert, called Madame Bovary. By the way, have you heard the good news? Napoleon made peace."

"No, I have not. Peace, what peace?"

"Where have you been? Napoleon declared war on Austrians in Italy. After the Battle of Solferino, he only made peace because he was alarmed by the unrest in Paris. There were heavy casualties, about 30,000 dead; which prompted Henri Dunant to campaign for establishing an organization called the International Red Cross."

"It is all, news to me. I have been traveling and have not seen a newspaper."

"You have not heard of the dauphine's death?" Monty shoke his head.

"He is buried at Chateau of Vaux-Renaud."

"According to the news, it is a good time for me to be immigrating to America."

"I heard America had a financial panic last year, but is slowly recovering. You know our French tightrope walker, Jean-Francois Gravelet is over there, and crossed Niagara Falls several times. We have reached Rennes. I get off here. Nice talking with you. I wish you well on your voyage. Au revoir."

Monty stepped from the coach, stretched his long legs and looked for facilities to relieve himself. Upon returning, he found three passengers seated in the coach. A French sailor, obviously headed for the coast. A peasant girl with an older lady, who was evidently her chaperone. The sailor had one too many drinks and quickly fell asleep. The girl stitched on handwork, while the older lady read. The girl sneaked a quick glance at Monty. He knew, not to speak to ladies until first they speak. The girl was beautiful, with sparkling blue eyes; not like Millie's eyes of faded, washed-out blue. It was hard to keep his eyes from straying her way. He gazed out the window, and again, in trance-like thought, returned to his isolated memories.

Daniel Pierre had been born the year the Camisards (Protestants in south France) rebelled against persecution from Louis XIV, and burned churches, killed or expelled priests. These were horrifying tales of a monarchy that responded with executions and burning of villages; and lasted three years with sporadic fighting another five years. It was the year Catherine I, a Lithuanian peasant, was captured during the Great Northern War and became the mistress of Peter the Great.

Stories began when Daniel was a babe, and the War of the Spanish Succession and Queen Anne's War were both in the second year of war. Daniel, as a youth, had wondered why John Zenger and two men in southwest Germany, who founded the Community of True Inspiration, immigrated to America. It was Daniel's first spurt of American curiosity. Monty recalled one story where Daniel laughed at The History of John Bull by John Arbuthnot showing a political cartoon of England as a stocky, countryman noted for honesty and stubborness. Tales were told about Daniel's cabinetry interest, and how he discovered Charles Cressent, whose colored-wood marquetry and ormolu and clever techique of applying gold dust into varnish, surpassed the old method of appling gold through the mercuric process that released poisionous fumes.

Monty remembered his grandpere Luke's way of telling Daniel's stories in dialogue. Told how Daniel at thirteen made his first bet, on wagers going around the village, on the sex of Charles de Beaumont. The story went, that Peter had said to Daniel, "Son, do you know what you are betting on?" After Daniel's answer, Pete replied, "That is not exactly right. Charles de Beaumont was a secret agent in the service of Louis XV's reign; and added, he did enjoy wearing women's clothes for disguises and for normal life."

His grandpere Luke had told Monty about George I, the first Hanoverian King of Great Britain and Ireland. A king who divorced his wife and imprisoned her for thirty-two years. A king of England, who never learned English and left government to his Whig ministers, who later saved him and his mistresses from disgrace over the South Sea Bubble scandal. Luke told Monty another story in dialogue.

Peter said to Daniel, "Son, the British market in South Sea stocks collapsed and affected many people in the colonies as well as the continent. Inquiry into this collapse revealed corruption of England's ministers and touched the king. Sir Robert Walpole came to the rescue by transferring stocks to the Bank of England and the East India Company. It was a case of the monarchy washing their dirty laundry."

Daniel then said, "Dad, he carried out important reforms, reorganized finances, built roads and encouraged commerce."

"Nonsense. All the work of Fleury. Louis XV is a puppet. He can not think unless Andre Fleury pulls his strings. Heavon help us if Fleury should die. The king would probably seek the counsel of his mistresses. Why he can not follow some of the good works of Frederick Willian I, I do not know."

"I agree, dad. All he has done for Prussia. It is strong and prosperous. He strengthened the army, passed financial reforms, and resettled the east. I think the most amazing feat is his freeing of serfs on his own domain and establishing compulsory primary education."

Monty went through the stories of scandals. The abusive relations of Peter the Great to his son, Alexis, who fled to Vienna to escape; only to be lured back by his father, who condemned Alexis to death for treason. Alexis had died before his scheduled execution.

The scandal of the Hotel de Soubise that belonged to the Rohan family. How Anne Chabot de Rohan, wife of Francois de Rohan managed favors from King Louis XIV and in return, understood her husband would became owner. Both died shortly after its remodeling. The mansion became the property of Hercule-Merdiadec Duc de Rohan-Rohan. A sixtyish duke and widower, who married a nineteen year old widow, Marie-Sophie de Courcillon.

The scandal of Catherine Bellier, the one-eyed, forty year old chambermaid, who initiated sixteen year old Louis XIV into the rites of love.

He remembered Daniel's favorite story, of the Procopio. The cafe that changed all cafes. Its style became so popular for cafes, they numbered three hundred at that time in Paris. How Daniel had studied Jean-Baptiste Bourguignon, geographer and cartographer, who improved the accuracy of maps, which further stirred his interest in America.

Often re-told and quoted, was the story of Daniel at thirty-one when the War of Polish Succession began. His dad had wept and asked, "Why did Fleury, who worked to maintain peace in Europe, get us involved in this war? Rival monarcial claimants over the Polish throne? Is that a principle? A Frenchman's cause for war? Will war ever be fought for an ideal, a principal, instead of greed?"

The darkness of night was conducive to reminiscing as Monty continued staring out the blackened window. A sudden whiff of briny sea air snapped him from his reverie. When the coach entered St. Brieuc, the noise of horse hoofs on cobblestones awakened the ladies and sailor.

"We must be here." The old lady said and politely covered her mouth as she yawned.

The sailor let the ladies and Monty descend from the carriage; hopped from the coach and sped away. Monty offered to help the ladies with luggage, but they refused. He took his bundle and asked directions for an inn. He had never seen such a pitch-black night. Fog hid everything and made it difficult to find his way.

"An extra charge if you plan to bathe." The innkeeper slapped a key on the desk.

Monty settled into bed and in the dark, drifted back to the comforting company of his olden stories. Daniel, in 1723, had a son--Lambert Andre de Regnier, called Andy. Daniel placed hopes upon the faint glimmer of a new enlightenment in France; one he hoped would begin for his son. Daniel brought the outside world into his hovel through the knowledge of reading. Thus, Andy learned of French art and the pastelist, Maurice-Quentin de La Tour and the famous people who sat for him--Voltaire, Madame de Pompadour, and Louis XV. It was said, Daniel did not place value on the books of the day, sentimental fictions of distress intended to arouse pity and compassion. Instead, he read Andy books inherited from his father; and spoke of the great musicians Handel, Bach, and Francois Philidor. It was said, Andy preferred tales about Charles Marie de La Condamine, who joined a geographical expedition to Peru and traveled down the Amazon River. Daniel curbed his son's adventureous nature by stressing story-examples, such as the Polish, Andrzej Zamoyski, who worked for parliamentary reform and the abolition of serfdom and freed his own serfs.

Monty recalled war broke out when Andy was sixteen, between England and Spain over commercial rivalry on the sea. England claimed Spanish mistreatment of sailors and Spain claimed the sailors were smugglers. The dispute erupted into the War of Jenkins Ear, and ended when Andy was twenty-five. Monty lay, thinking of the wars that continued through each generation, and fell asleep.

He awakened early and ate a breakfast of pancakes and porridge. He asked directions to the docks, and found the building housing travel agents selling package deals that included ship passage and train travel.

"You are telling me the next Cunard Line is not sailing for a month?"

"That is right. There are freighters and cargos out there."

Monty left to look for a freighter leaving today. After asking several captains, he found a freighter sailing the next morning.

"Over there, pier seven. Pay your ticket and board." The burly captain continued walking the dock, seeking passengers. Monty approached pier seven where a crowd of immigrants were paying for tickets and boarding. The gray sky intensified the bleakness that shown in the immigrants' faces; most in tattered rags that showed the signs of their long, dangerous journey to reach this point.

"This here is a freighter, son. We only have steerage passage."

"One ticket for passage. No railroad fare."

"Roundtrip?"

"No. You are selling many tickets. Can you carry all these people?"

"Do not worry about our business. You want to go to America. Right?"

Monty gave him no answer, but boarded the gangplank. He joined the group standing on deck, but there was no room to walk among those on board. The deck's railing was packed with people idly watching the water below. Fathers and mothers held babies, excited children squeezed between adults and clusters of families tried to remain together. The din was ear-shattering, voices in different tongues, and all in the high pitch of anticipation. The noise, like a flock of raucous birds roosting in a tree, droned on. When the last passenger boarded and the gangplank raised, the crowd gave boisterous cheers.

"You may sleep on deck tonight. Those preferring to go to steerage compartment, go now. We will lock the doors at night. Tomorrow we sail, and all of you will go to steerage at night." The captain ordered and quickly disappeared.

Many, like Monty, had no idea how cold the seacoast night could be. Families huddled together, babies cried, and the old moaned. Monty thought he would walk to stir up body heat, but there was no room among the sleeping bodies. Morning did not come for one old man, who had died from the cold.

The gangplank went down with a bang. The captain was furious his sailing schedule was delayed. The crowd somberly watched, as the dead man's body was transported from the ship.

"You may stay on deck or go below. Thirteen knots, and you must all enter steerage, if the weather becomes bad." Shouted the captain.

Monty stayed on deck as the ship sailed from port out to sea. In the dense overcast of fog, there was no sea to see. No horizon to behold. No sky to mark his bearings. As the ship headed out to sea, pangs of doubt surfaced with each lapping wave. He stood in stunned wonder at the lack of visibility; gloomy feelings of desolation filled his being. The foggy, blinding space seemed to create a stoppage of time. He felt alone, engulfed in foggy space. A haunting emptiness, isolation, and fear enveloped him as real as the shrouding, saturating fog. Monty had not seen the captain arrive with his men, but heard his command.

"All below, come to deck at once if you want breakfast." Slowly the able steerage passengers lumbered up the steps. Monty did not see those remaining below; unable to make it up the steps.

"Form a line to the right." Ordered the captain. His two officers handed out cups to the first ten passengers in line. "After you drink, pass your cup on to the next person." One shipmate dipped a cup into a container of water, while the other officer dipped into a vat of milk. The captain handed each passenger a sourdough roll.

Leaning against the deck rail, Monty tried blocking out the present with the past. He had gone as far as Andy, who married Marie Elizabeth Cartier and gave birth to Peter Antoine de Regnier II, but could not think any further. After vomiting overboard, he headed down the steps to steerage. A hundred more people were below, huddling together without light or fresh air and trying to stay warm from the six inches of sea water on the floor. They wallowed in filth, and breathed the fetid atmosphere. The fevered ill lay between the healthy, in places so narrow it denied a change of position.

Monty started back up the steps and stopped to ask a man near the doorway, "When did you people board the ship?"

"We boarded two days before sailing."

The captain had deliberately put the first group into steerage, so as not to be seen. It became clear to Monty, the freighter not only hauled freight, but also carried the money-making human cargo--immigrants. The captain did not care about the living or dying. He had their passage money and the convenience of sea burials. Monty returned to the deck, mad and helpless.

Monty had asked himself, before breakfast and before his thoughts had wondered, how this predicament began? This mass of helpless people. Helplessly forced to endure the conditions of one man's profiteering. The hazy vapors held his eyes sightless, but his mind was not in a foggy state. In Monty's mind, no fog obscured the captain's state of greed. Monty stared into the cloudy murkiness and hypnotic nothingness, and sighed, "Greed, is everywhere." In the damp, shadowy screen before him, he tried pushing the captain's greed out of his mind, but his thoughts drifted back to the profiteering of kings and profit seeking officials, who had plagued his ancestors. He recalled the story of another Attester.

CHAPTER 2: ANOTHER ATTESTER

"Merci, born according to Hoyle." Announced Lambert Andre, nick-named Andy, who joyfully clasped his hands. He stood a head taller than his father, Daniel; but today felt he towered upward into the heavons. He was a daddy.

"You finally learned the rules." Said Daniel. The men chuckled, sharing the current idiom from Edmond Hoyle's popular English book on the rules and authority for card games.

It was two years into the War of the Austrian Succession and life for the French peasantry was dominated by rules and authority according to the king. A time when monarcial rule, when not obeyed, meant decapitation, hanging, or being burned alive, according to the crime or social status. The somber, grave times seldom allowed moments of humor. The peasants had latched on to this idiom as a satirical and humorous innuendo to gleefully imply, not everything went according to the king.

"How is Marie doing?" Asked Daniel.

"Very well; having him baptized the day after tomorrow."

Father Moreau and the priest before him, were well aware of the Regniers. Each generation had hoodwinked priests into academic lessons and catechism for their children. The countryside was filled with peasants of large families. Peter Antoine II, was the only child of Marie and Andy.

Daniel tilted his head, lowered it so his eyes strained upwards and peered into Andy's eyes. He stroked his chin, and asked, "Son, what is his name?"

Andy hesitated, did dad expect a namesake? "Peter Antoine II, after his great grandpere." Daniel uttered in glee, "Peter Antoine, you say. That is our family attester. Wonderful, son. Will please Maggie. Come to the table. Let us celebrate with a game of whist, since you know the rules."

"You ladies going to join us?" Diane helped Daniel's mother, Maggie, to a table bench, "Mom are you comfortable?"

"Oui." Maggie was feeble and despondent since Peter, her husband, had died. Diane settled herself on a bench near the table. "It is nice, there is now a card game where women are allowed to play."

Fear and worry filled today and the tomorrows. Britain's fight with Spain, the War of Jenkin's Ear, continued into the War of the Austrian Succession. Britain's support of Austria resulted in Spain becoming France's only ally against Prussia. The mood of the country was grave as Frederick the Great II made Prussia into a major European power. French spirits were filled with emotional conflicts; further aggravated by their famed countryman, Voltaire, who was gathering around and sharing artistic talents with Frederick the Great. Monarcies were at odds. Major European countries were fighting for no cause but greed, for control and power.

The peasants held little interest in the conflict between Britain and France, over who would control North America. They lived in the impact of war's on-going suffering. America was in its third French and Indian war, King George's War. In Europe it was called the War of the Austrian Succession and involved most nations through a hodgepodge of alliances. North American tribal Indians were fighting over land, and slaves were revolting for liberty. In South America, the last descendant of the Inca emperor, Amaru Tupac, led a revolution for freedom against Spanish rule. It was a time of worldwide cries, uprisings, war dances, and warfare.

At sunset, Daniel returned from visiting neighbors and sauntered into the hovel. Daniel saw Andy reading by the hearth's firelight. He skipped over and gave his son's shoulder a proud slap. Andy shut his book. "Dad, what neighbors were you boasting, bragging, and boring to death?"

Daniel burst forth a few snorts and picked up the book to see what Andy was reading. "Never you mind. They were as jubilant as I, over our blessed event, and asked time of the baptismal ceremony. I said, after Sunday's Mass. Then Francis Trudeau returned from the village, and said she had heard some of the shops planned on closing to attend the ceremony."

"All this time you were at Phillip's home?"

"Phillip poured wine and his wife brought in crackers. Even shared some snuff. Was I supposed to drink, eat, and then run like a dog?"

"Mom simply asked me where you were."

"My Diane, she is as flighty as a butterfly since Peter arrived. Can not keep her mind on anything. I told her I was going to the neighbors."

"You know Diane and great grandmere, have been busy planning the ceremony. Now it is here. Bound to be nervous. You know how women are. It is good to see Maggie in better spirits. By the way, how did Phillip come to have snuff?"

"Found the box on the roadside near his home. Figured it fell from an aristocrat's carriage on his way to Paris."

Daniel's mood turned serious. "Now, about this ceremony thing? It is going to be big. Everybody is interested in Peter's birth. Do not know how far the word has spread. I know it has spread in the village. I realize people consider it a miracle, your years of childless marriage are over, but the curious are apt to appear. People we do not know."

"Dad, it is a miracle and a blessing. Diane said we have been assured of parish help. Mom told me Father Moreau said during these worrisome times, people need to look forward to a joyful festivity. Parish women will be bringing food, the men wines, and what our women have planned, should take care of the people. Do not worry."

Daniel kicked at the sod floor. "Can not see the why, of all this fuss. It is our family affair. All those people clamoring, drinking, and celebrating, in no time, there will be suspicious Royal Guards upon us, arresting and suspecting us of a treasonable meeting or inciting a mob. You know it has been happening everywhere."

"Dad, you always told me, blessings should be shared."

Daniel was not to be enlightened, "Son, blessings paint rosy pictures. The world, is it not a blessing? Look at the mess man has done, and is doing. It has been over eighty years since France was at its zenith. Life and conditions have not improved."

Peter's first year of life was filled with reaching, crawling and walking eagerly into his future. Where would his steps go? Peter's wee soles grew, while monarchism grew and crushed, splintered, ravaged the land and its people's souls. Neither Peter's feet, nor feet of the masses would be able to walk away from the impelling future. Monarchs reached for more and more. All of Europe became embroiled in reaching, lusting, and warring. Archduchess Maria Theressa, after father's death, walked into her reign amidst monarchical claimants lusting for her throne. King Frederick II of Prussia crawled into east-central Europe grabbing Silesia from Austria to gain more wealth and power.

The year was 1746, and after a weary day's work, the family gathered for supper. Daniel took to his rocker and lit the pipe Andy had carved for him. Andy sat in the rocker Daniel had made him last

Christmas, before Maggie had died. "Dad, when I was in for tobacco, Mr. Bouteau talked about England's Bonnie Prince Charlie (Charles Edward Stuart) escaping to exile in Europe. What do you think?"

"Not surprised. Lack of support cost him the Battle at Culloden. Where do you suppose he ran?"

"Certainly not to Scotland or England. Maybe here?"

"No, I would bet on Switzerland."

Daniel thought for awhile before speaking, "While in the tavern, John Dumier . . ., you know the hatter who is always talking about coffee houses he frequents on trips to Paris, started a rumpus when he said the city in America, called New York, had only two coffee-houses."

"Why the rumpus?"

"Because, it brought up the subject of America. Villagers are angry and talking about our fight with England over control of America. David Portier was in the tavern. His son, Eugene, is in our military over there. He is quite concerned since he heard a colonial force led by a Massachusetts governor, William Shirley, had captured our fortress of Louisbourg and deported 6000 neutral, Acadian farmers because of their French ancestry."

Daniel soberly shoke his head back and forth. "Poor David, he has cause to worry. I read a tribe of Indians called Iroquois are fighting with the colonists. Colonists left to get away from monarchism. Can not blame them for fighting for independence. I think it was in Poor Richard's Almanak, that I read colonists now number around 890,000. I can not understand about the Indian fights. Etienne de Condillac wrote, 'All knowledge springs from senses and association of ideas.' Which, I dare say, to me, means, I would have to live in America to have any understanding of the crisis of the Indian tribes."

At age five, Peter recovered from a serious illness and was not among the numbered losses. The village had 53 deaths from the war, 16 from starvation, 7 imprisoned and executed, 11 from sweating sickness, 9 from old age and 4 from giving birth to new French citizens. The village population was slowly dwindling. The next year brought continuing death, higher tailles and larger harvest portions being taken for the army, which left farmers with meager amounts for survival.

"Dad, I took a couple of my carved pipes into the tobacco shop and sold them. Almost bought a book I saw in one shop. Then, I wondered if we had our taille saved. Do we?"

"Yes. We have almost finished the savings. What book did you see?"

"I saw two. Our reading to Peter has taught him alot, but I intend to ask the priest if he can begin teaching him. He is six and has a vivid curiosity about books. The books I saw were Don Quixote and The Vicar of Wakefield."

"Son, he could not possibly read those."

"I know, dad, but this German engraver, Daniel Chodowiecki, did marvelous etchings in both books. I know Peter would enjoy the pictures. It would tempt him to read them later."

"I would like to see those, myself. Buy them."

Peter had childhood heartaches from disappointments, but nothing prepared him for the loss of his great grandmere Maggie. She was his constant refuge after every scolding. She was at his bedside during his illness. She had been there to sympathize and wipe his tears. "Why did great grandmere die?" Marie wrapped both arms around him, "There is no answer to the why of death, son. Her heart wore out." Andy, hoping to change the subject, said, "Now eat your porridge and boiled buttermilk. Need your help in reaping the north field. Your mom wants those wild plums in the woods picked before they disappear."

"Where is grandpere?"

"Dad is at the cemetery visiting his mother's grave, and for awhile he will not be working with us. He will be going there often."

"Why does he go there so many times?"

"His soul hurts. Visiting grandmere's grave eases his pain. Understand?" Peter looked quizzically at Andy. "Is that what hurts inside me? Soul? What you told me about that Moses man?"

"Yes. Moses Mendelsshon. He wrote about the immortality of the soul and the existence of a personal God? Understand?"

"No. Do not understand. I miss great grandmere."

Andy again tried to change the subject, and patted Peter's hand. "Take your scythe and go out and work the north field. I will join you soon. Son, next time I go to the village, I will bring back a surprise for you." Andy had not finished eating when he heard Peter's hollering. "Voila, Voila. Good news. Viola, Voila." He ran towards home, flinging his arms and swirling the scythe in circles above his tousled, red hair.

"Marie, what is Peter screaming about?" She hesitantly opened the hovel's upper-half door. Shaking her head, she shut the door quickly as early October air was brisk and cold. "He is not hurt, just running towards the house shouting." She resumed her daily labors. "Andy, you have to do something about Peter's speech. He is six and should know better. When happy, he shouts. When sad, he whimpers. Otherwise, he speaks in a monotone."

"Some things take time. He will grow out of it. I will see what he is roaring about." Andy cast his leatherwork aside, when in burst Peter. "Did you hear?"

"Son, you are always roaring and bellowing."

"War is over, Dad. The eggman hollered to me from the road. Hear the bell tolling?"

"Think I am going to faint." Whispered Marie, and sped from the wash-chest to a nearby chair. That is why the bell is tolling; not because someone died." She walked to an opened window shutter to stare into space. Andy staggered and flopped into his rocker. Everyone was silent and wondering, after nine years, can the War of Austrian Succession be over?

"Daddy, help momma?"

"No, son."

"Why not?"

"It is shock. She is all right. When war finally ends, it is a miracle one can not quickly believe. Peter, go tell your grandpere the news. He is at the cemetery."

It was October 18, 1748, the signing of the Treaty of Aix-la Chapelle. Across the entire continent, nighttime was strewn with grateful thanks, tears and universal prayers. The church bell toller climbed the three flights of stairs to the church attic and ascended the ladder into the belfry to toll the bell constantly until midnight, ringing out the news the war had ended. Too many times the bell had tolled, ringing five times if a male had died, four times for a female, or three times if under age eighteen. The toll then followed with rings for each year of the deceased's life. The peasants knew to count slowly to five between each ring and with a double pause before counting the toll for the years. Bell tolling was a frequent occurrence and seldom heeded since there were so many deaths.

Peter knew better than to interrupt dad or grandpere while working in the field. He knew his questions, unless emergencies, were to wait until after the evening meal. Peter heard adult talk about the war, and now he had a question. Waiting filled Peter with anxiety and accelerated energy. He swathed with a vengeance at the dried sheaths. Time dragged when he had to contain his curiosity and wait until the sun drug itself into sunset. When would the family finish supper? At last, he could ask. "I want to know, why we have war?"

"My son, the questioner. I am surprised at you. The answer is in one word--greed. Remember your history? Templars and the Hospitallers? Even the orders of knighthood could not get along among themselves. It is the people of 'ton' who make war, while the simple people bleed."

Marie wanted no more war talk. "Son, get ready for bed. Tomorrow is another day of labors. Work must be done before the rain sets in."

"I know, but about war..."

Andy cut in saying, "Peter, that is enough. Off to bed." Marie was glaring at him. Daniel noticed an argument brewing, and motioned for Diane to head for the bedroom. "Think we will bed down."

"You should not be so abrupt. He is only a boy of seven. A boy who thinks and needs answers."

"I know. I know. My fears make me angry."

"Fears? What are you talking about?"

"Now, Marie, you do not fool me. You are worried, too. Face it. If another war breaks out, it will not be long before Peter will be old enough to be conscripted."

"Let us keep the joy and beauty of childhood within his life as long as we can."

Andy hit his fist upon the table, "Not on my life. That is the problem. He is too idealistic. I have been trying to decide when, and how, to start rubbing the dirt of reality into him. Someday, his survival may depend upon facing certainties that exist." Marie began weeping. Andy bent over and caressed her henna hair. "You cry, but do not try to escape and run from reality. Life is a toughening process." Marie tried controlling her emotion, but words came out between sobs. "What? What can? What can we do?" Andy lovingly reached for her hand and gently stroked it, "My Marie, for starters the next time we have chicken, do not kill the hen. Peter will. I will speak to him and work with him. Guide him into helping dad and I butcher. It is a matter of conditioning. He will be up to it after our talk."

Marie was relieved the task would not be hers. "Tomorrow, I am walking to the parish library to see if there isn't another book of Carlo Goldoni's plays. Comedy takes my mind off woes and worries."

"Marie, you would not believe the chatter in the village." Said Andy.

"Another new courtesan of the court?" Sighed Marie.

"No, they talked about Maria Gaetana Agnesi. She has been appointed at Bologna University. Job Matlin from the bookstore, said she was a child prodigy in mathematics. A woman? A woman appointed to the university? Can you believe it?"

"Why not? We have brains and skills. What about Rosalba Carriera, the Italian painter? She showed all Paris how to use pastels. You brilliant men had nothing else to discuss?"

Diane was doing her stitchery until her laughter forced her to set it aside. "Merci, Marie, my laughter is exhausting me." Andy raised an eyebrow, and said, "We talked about Samuel Johnson in England, who is producing a weekly paper. Josua Corrine at the fish market and Job, both paid a traveler selling the paper, to bring them copies. The tavern group turned on Dave and Job, blasting them for buying an English paper."

"Surely, those brilliant men did not behave foolishly."

"You are pretty persnickety today, dear. It did not bother Dave or Job one bit. He said it would bring him customers. After an ale or two, I walked to the fish market to read Josua's copy, as all those brilliant men were hovering over Job's paper."

"What is the paper called?"

"The Rambler."

Peter became skilled with the crossbow and quivers his dad made for his tenth birthday. Peter no longer had to throw rocks at the birds that gobbled the dropped seeds during planting season. A bird felled from his arrow scared the flock away for a longer period of time.

Andy wiped sweat from his brow, hoeing in the dried field was taxing. "Dad, I agree with the Scotchman, Adam Smith. He writes a peasant should be free within the law to promote his own interests; which in turn promotes the interest of the masses. Do you agree?"

Daniel stepped to close the gap between himself and Andy, and angrily kicked the dirt. "Dream talk. Never talk to outsiders or villagers, of such things. You could be arrested. Hear me, son?" There was silence as Andy continued hoeing and Daniel followed, planting seedlings. "How did you learn about Smith?"

"At the smitty's, Francois Bonet, said a customer came in who had heard Smith lecture."

"You heed my words. You hear, son?"

"Dad, are you feeling all right? Are you upset."

"I am as fit as an ox. Upset? Yes. War may be ended, but monarchies and unrest still threaten. While gathering wood, I met our new neighbor to the northeast, Joseph Kaunitz. He and his family were on their way to the village, when he saw me and stopped. Mighty fearful, he was. He did not want anyone to see us talking. I asked, 'why not?' His story is incredible. Originally, he lived on a farm on the east side of Paris. Royal Guards came one day and presented 'lettres de cachet,' the judicial orders issued by the king. At the moment, Joseph feared the arrest had something to do with his name. He told the guards he was not related to Count von Wenzel Kaunitz. Since the guards did not know of the count, he knew the arrest was about something else. The guards did not explain, and arrested his eldest son without a trial and executed him. Joseph feared our talking could bring me trouble. That son, is the state of affairs now existing in France. I fear it will get worse."

As did most twelve year old French boys, Peter secretly thought of joining the military. War was raging over four continents. The French and Indian war continued. Famous French men volunteered and crossed the sea to America.

"Dad, do you believe in Jean Rousseau's view?"

"Which one?"

"Man's nature is spoiled by corrupt society? Or does the affects of war spoil man?"

"You have started reading my books, eh?"

"No. Lessons with Father Moreau."

"No. Man's nature is spoiled by imperfect monachism that corrupts itself and society."

"Why?"

"Need you ask? We live in its results--oppression, taxes, and graft."

"Rousseau is a famous thinker. I would like to be a thinker." Andy smiled dotingly over his growing son. "He is a philosopher. Someday, you may also be a good one."

Peter's questions at thirteen were more taxing. He liked to sit on a footstool beside Daniel, while they read. "Grandpere, I do not understand this. These big words? What do they mean?" He pointed to the part he did not understand. Daniel took the book and read the passage aloud. "'There is an absolute moral law, which can never be modified by expediency and the obligation to obey this moral law is called the categorical imperative binding upon every rational human being.'"

"Does that Jesuit have you reading Kant?" Asked Andy.

Not wanting his question dismissed, Peter again asked, "Grandpere, what does it mean?"

"That means, Kant believes it can never be right, to tell a lie." A smirk of disdain formed upon Peter's face. "I know that. Why doesn't he say that?"

"Guess, it is his highbrow German. Perhaps, he thinks a philosopher should use mammoth words." Daniel replied, hoping to end his questions. "I am reading about our Marquis de Montcalm's battles in America." Peter knew the Marquis was grandpere's hero.

"Son, Sam Johnson, who writes the Rambler, has printed a dictionary. I will buy you one, next trip to the village."

"The first word I look up, will be expediency."

"Dad, how is the Marquis doing? Running the British out? Asked Andy.

"He captured Fort Oswego and laid siege to Fort William Henry. I can not believe the number of Indian tribes, who have joined us: Iroquois, Creek, Choctaw and Cherokee. How many do you suppose is in a tribe?"

Marie gave a puzzling look, "How can they tell them apart?"

"Who cares. Let me finish my reading," said Daniel.

CHAPTER 3: BEAST AND MAN

Monty was tiring, leaning against the deck rail, and seated himself below; threw his arms over the middle rail for safety and dangled his feet from the deck. He vomited again. Time passed slowly. Time went more quickly pursuing resurrected memories. He thought of a story told him of a 1756 springtime, when danger befell Andy.

Andy would dispell his worries of war with walks amidst nature's beauty and renewal; where nature showed her colorful green arrangement and design. He leisurely walked through the woods until he noticed a mossy rock with bits of spotted gray moss dying from the lingering, longer days of sunshine. Andy thought of his grandmere, Maggie, and remembered her feisty ways and the muscles on her wiry frame. As she aged, her days were spotted with naps that became frequent and longer, until her eternal rest. He thought of his dad, who claimed to be as fit as an ox. He had spotted times when Daniel's right arm caused him difficulty? Andy glanced again at the clump of soft moss and tears burned his weathered cheeks. Time is spotted with the signs of dying and death.

Jacque had walked to Andy's to spread the news and met Peter outside the stable. "Britain has declared war on France." Said Jacque. Peter was expected to walk and notify their neighbor of the news, but first, he sped to tell his dad, who was plowing in the field.

Andy left the plow-share embedded in the sod, removed the yoke from ol' Ox, and headed to the house. Ol' Ox obediently followed towards the stable's open door. He wondered how would he break the news to Diane and Marie? Upon entering the room, his emotions took over. "Damn, Frederick the Great. Ghoul of Prussia. He started this whole mess by seizing Silesia."

"What are you roaring about?" Marie, pulled up a chair for him, "Sit, I will fix you a hot cup of tea. Then we talk."

"Britain and France are at war." Startled, Marie dropped her coveted Wedgwood cup, a wedding gift sent from an English friend. "Merci," she exclaimed and sat herself in the nearest chair.

"Saw it coming." In a daze, Daniel shifted his rocker slowly. The commotion awakened Diane from her nap and she wandered from the bedroom. Marie rose to help her to a chair, "Mom, France is at war."

Peter was fourteen, that day of May 15, 1756. The war had worldwide scope and started with Austria's desire to regain Silesia and Prussia's invasion of Saxony. France, Austria, Russia and Spain were at war against Prussia, Britain, and Hanover.

Peter entered breathlessly and sat down. "Son, did you tell the Gautier family the news?" "Yes, they were in the fields. Coming home, I thought I saw ol' Ox down the road, further south. Could not tell exactly. Is he in the stable?"

Andy realized it could be ol' Ox, and jumped up to check the stable. "Gone. I have to go after him."

"I will go, dad."

"No. You rest. You had a hefty run to the Gautier's." Grandpere Daniel had been quietly rocking. The news was a shock. Too fast to comprehend. He was becoming rattled. He did not want ol' Ox lost. "I know where he is. I will find ol' Ox."

"No dad, you are in no condition to ramble around in the woods."

"Wonder how Ox strayed?" Diane plaintively asked.

"I see the stable door is ajar. I must have forgotten to shut it."

"I noticed the plow in the field. I will finish plowing. Dad, don't forget the goad."

Andy hastily walked south on the road, peering into the woods on either side. At times he chuckled, at times composed, and repeated the ditties as he sang and stepped to the cadence. "You bloated old desperado. Desequilibre, desequilibre." He spotted ol' Ox munching on green underbrush and routed him onto the road.

A short distance ahead the road made a bend. He had the goad ready in case ol' Ox bolted from the road. Ox and man neared the bend, when suddenly a calvary troop came racing around the bend. The line of horses spread the width of the road. Horse hooves trampled rocks and dirt, and thrust clouds of thick lingering dust. Andy had given ol' Ox a swat, but was unable to clear himself from the road. The elite, uniformed cavalry raced onward without a single change of gait. The troops could not be delayed by a mere, fallen peasant.

Andy lay with one shattered leg upon the roadway. He sat up and saw a proturding bone in his leg and the other leg with flesh wounds. He reached to break a branch from a bordering bush to use as a splint, but passed out from pain. Ol' Ox had not left, but nudged his ringed nostrils into the ground near Andy's head to awaken him. Andy stroked ol' Ox's jowls, his loyal presence was comforting. Ol' Ox shifted his bulky form into a laying position beside Andy, and the two rested on the roadside.

Peter saw his mother running across the field and left the plow to hurry towards her. "Something wrong?"

"It is dad. He is not back, yet."

"I will look for him." Peter ran down the road, faster and faster. He tried to dismiss his perturbing thoughts. Was dad lost roaming into the woods? Had some roving ruffians emerged from the woods; attacked him and stolen ol' Ox? Around the bend Peter saw them laying together near the ditch. He sighed in relief. Then he saw Andy's crumpled leg.

"My God, dad. This is terrible. Do not talk. Just rest while I try to put your leg back in place." Peter stripped a green twig from a bush and handed it to Andy. "Bite on this, it will hurt." Peter yanked once and the exposed bone slid back in place. He splinted the leg with his sweaty, ripped, strips of cloth torn from his shirt. "Do not move. I will get the cart."

"Take ol' Ox with you."

"No dad, he is too slow." Peter raced back and into the house. He sat for a brief rest and explained the crisis. Diane hysterically sobbed, sputtering, "My son. My poor son." Daniel put his arm around her, "Do not have a tizzy. Everyone is upset."

Peter left to pull the cart in front of the stable and picked up the yoke. Marie ran outside, "Peter you take that side. I will take this side."

"Here, let me do that." Daniel stood in the doorway.

"No. You stay with Diane. Try to calm her." Together, Peter and Marie pulled the cart down the road. Ol' Ox pulled the cart and the three, back home. Inside, Andy was placed in a chair, his sprinted leg rested upon a plank placed from his chair to a footstool.

"Diane, now you just keep quiet." Ordered Daniel.

Peter retrieved a jug of fermented cider from the root cellar. "Here, mom, heat this. It will relax him." Marie poured the cider into a small pot and hung it over the fire, and hastened to cover Andy's leg with vinegar, and poured and poured.

"Woman, that is enough. It is running on the floor."

"Hush. Your other leg wound needs attention."

Not evident was Andy's inner turmoil. His false pride pained him from fear of being handicapped. He thought of his old friend, Jacque, who had lost a leg in the war of the Polish Succession and his humor returned. "Pshaw. Do not know why you are fussing around. Peter, you find me a good hickory stick, tomorrow. One I can carve into a cane. A cane far-fancier than Jacque's."

"Sure thing dad. First thing tomorrow. Do not worry about farmwork, you know I can handle it. You still want potatoes planted in the southwest corner?"

"Damn right." Andy was quick to notice Marie did not hush his cussing and so continued, "Get the hell trampled out of you on the road. Next thing you know, they will damn well be plundering our house, food, and livestock. Damn wars. Damn monarchs."

Marie tried to pacify him. "I have a nice larder hidden in our root cellar."

"You have? What have you stashed away?"

"Dried peas, onions, beets, and yams."

"Yams? Where did you get yams?"

"Last February, I took a loaf of bread to Louise Richelieu, Jacque's wife, and we visited awhile. She gave me some tubers. I intended to keep it a secret and surprise you on a cold winter day."

"How do you like that? Mom, the sneak."

It had been five years since Daniel had told Andy the Kaunitz story. Now, both men realized who Count von Wenzel Kaumitz was--the Austrian Chancellar, who controlled foreign policy under Empress Marie Theresa. The Count's influence had revised the European alliances of the War of Austrian Succession and made France and Russia allies.

When Peter reached fifteen, he grew wise to the wiles of women. He relished discussions with his dad over scandals of Mme. de Pompadour and other courtesans of the Court. He enjoyed talking about heros. Grandpere Daniel's hero was the popular General Marquis de Montcalm, who regained control of Ontario for France, only to die defending Quebec. Peter's hero was Francois Quesnay, who headed a group of French economists called physiocrats. Peter believed as Quesnay, France's real producers were farmers, like himself; and merchants were secondary, merely processors, to his country's needs. It fell in place with the Adam Smith lectures. Beliefs that boosted Peter's self-pride.

The snow stopped falling as the year 1758 arrived. Woods were covered with white strokes of puffy snow clinging to the tree branches. The hovel was boarded up and dark. Candle light flickered as Peter finished his breakfast of hot porridge. "Dad, what are your plans for today? Do you need me around this morning?"

"We have two barrels of soil collected before the ground froze, sitting in the stable corner. Figured, with this snow, the women could melt it and we can mix a batch of mud and straw to chauk the walls. There are several cracks and places letting in cold. Did you have something in mind?"

"Yes. Tracking would be good. I would like to go hunting."

Marie sat her mug of buttermilk down, "Oh my, a rabbit would be nice for supper."

"That is what I had in mind, Mom. The hides on the north windows are tattered and no longer keep out drafts. It is time to tack up new pelts." Peter bundled into his wrappings and reached for his crossbow and quivers. "Son, later we will begin doing some practice shooting with my gun." Peter had left, when Andy said to Daniel, "The kid's aim is better than yours or mine."

"He seems to prefer his crossbow to the gun. Guns" Muttered Diane.

"What about them?" Asked Daniel.

"All the killing going on. Then to read about more. It is upsetting to me. I picked up the Rambler the other day. Gun battles. Fort Louisbourg fell. Indian tribes switching to the British side. All the killing. It is done with guns, and it is upsetting."

"You mean the warring in America? Yes, it does look as though the tide has turned in favor of England. Since they put William Pitt in charge of foreign affairs, they are getting the better of us."

"Talk about something else?" Diane suggested.

"Our women would rather hear gossip. Do you have any?"

"You bet. Our ambassador to Vienna, Duc de Etienne Choiseul, has been going back and forth negotiating the marriage of Marie Antoinette to Louis XVI. Playing cupid, I suppose."

"An Austrian?" Diane gasped. Marie added, "She is a mere child of three years."

Andy kicked Daniel's foot under the table. "Guess, our womenfolk did not like your gossip."

Peter returned from his hunt empty handed; supper was limited to the usual. "Peter, bring the slice of hanging lamb-jerky to the table?" Marie placed sugar in her mouth, and then sipped her tea without milk. She placed the cup down. "Andy, did you know Peter is in his third puppy love?"

"Another? Three, by age sixteen? Who is this one?"

"Oh, mom, I would appreciate a little privacy."

"He wants privacy. I would say it sounds serious, eh mom? What is her name?"

"Elisa. I met her when she was buying bread at the bakery."

"Does that mean she can not bake bread?"

"Oh, dad, I am not going to say anymore about her." Peter did not mind dad's laughter, but mom's bothered him. He finished his bread and butter and left to begin changing from chore clothes into his church garb.

"Marie, what is going on? Is he getting ready for church without being told?"

Marie, smiled knowingly. "Yes, dear. Elisa belongs to our parish."

CHAPTER 4: KEEPER OF THE PATH

Monty heard seasick passengers vomiting and saw them cringing over the deck rail. He scrambled over, dizzy from his sickness, to sit upon wooden planks. Recollections had amused and occupied his time, and temporarily kept his mind off his sea sickness. He continued delving in a review of unfolding memories.

Peter was seventeen and capable of working the homestead. The hard farm labor was now up to him, as Andy was crippled and Daniel no longer could manage laborous tasks. Working alone, he would fantasize about Elisa.

"Time for lunch." Marie leaned across the half-door and waited for a reply. At the doorway, Peter brushed off the dust from the field and entered, grabbing a rafter and chinning himself in masculine glory. He walked over to his dad, resting in his rocker. "What are you reading?"

"I was reading Mes Reveries.

"Oh, is it about courtesan lovers?"

"It is a book you should read. Or has love blinded you to knowledge?" Peter enjoyed his dad's wit and humor, but this remark was not made in jest.

Diane said slyly, "Grandad and I were married at sixteen."

"Diane, what was the purpose of saying that?" Scowled Daniel.

Marie said, "Your grandpere is in a bad mood, since learning Marquis Montcalm was killed. The battle cost 1400 French soldiers. We only hope, Eugene Portier is not among the dead." Andy made no comment on the bad news. Something bothered him. Peter realized his coming eighteenth birthday preyed heavily upon his mind. "What is that book about, dad?"

Before answering, Andy poured vinegar over his garden greens, took a bite of bread and drank his buttermilk. Thoughts lingered in his mind over his mother's comment--"married at sixteen."

"It is about warfare, from Maurice, Comte de Saxe. He was one of our marshals who fought in the army. Being so inclined about romance, you might like to know he was the illegitimate son of Augustus the Strong of Poland." Peter noticed dad's verbal, empathic pronunciation upon the word, strong, and understood its implication. Dad's humor was back. Now would be the time to ask.

"Can I invite Elisa for Sunday dinner?" An awkward silence lingered. "I will kill the chicken." Andy and Marie burst into laughter. Marie managed to muster, "Oui," between her laughter. Peter hid his startled expression by eyeing his bowl of porridge. He wondered, why his remark was funny?

Sunday dinner with Elisa was the highlight of Peter's young life. Her presence cast his old world into a new light. Elisa's delight over the cidar, flattered Andy. Elisa's shyness pleased Marie. And Diane, his grandmother was as contented as a mother hen.

"You lost your father at five? What happened, was your father in the war?" Asked Andy.

"Hush. Maybe she would rather not talk about it." Marie scolded.

"Oh, I enjoy speaking about him, least I become like my mother. She reminds me of the French legend, the fairy tale of Mellusine."

Peter had never heard the legend, "Lisa, what is it about?"

Elisa, sat back in her chair, pleased she knew something Peter did not. "Mellusine, the fairy, was punished by being changed into a serpent from her waist down, but it happened only on Saturdays. Mellusine's husband broke his promise to not see her on a Saturday. When he showed up one Saturday, she vanished. It is said her cries were heard at Lusignan castle before the death of each of her descendants."

"Why does that seem like your mother?" Asked Marie.

Elisa gently folded her hands upon the table. "Because she has imprisoned herself. Mother seldom moves. Just sits and weaves, day after day. Dad was an officer in the aristocratic military. I was born in Austria and when Frederick the Great of Prussia seized Silesia, dad wanted to escape to France. But mother did not. When he was killed, then Mom insisted on moving here. Her older siblings moved to other provinces. I remember dad taught me to dance."

The visit with Peter's parents was the highlight of Elisa's life. After questions and dinner conversation ebbed, Andy picked up a book and settle himself in his wooden rocker. "Here, this beautiful day shines upon us, why not go for a walk?"

"Let us go." Said Peter, and wasted no time in taking Elisa's hand and heading outside.

Marie turned from stacking plates to peer at Andy until he glanced up. "I think your remark was a bit rude, as though you wanted them out?" Andy did not wish to face Marie with his answer; he bent his head towards his book as he spoke. "Perhaps. But I am praying for nature to take its course. If he marries soon and has a child before going to war."

"Merciful heavons. You men." Marie shook her head.

Peter guided Elisa to a vantage point where the farm came into full view. She gazed at the countryside. "The farm is like a scene from le Nain family painters. How long has your family lived here?"

"Do not know. From stories told to me, it was during fuedal times when the family first began paying the taille for working the baron's land. Somewhere along the lineage were descendants of King Charlamagne, so land was granted with lowered taille to the head of the family. Mathurin Regnier was a notable poet in the 1600's, and added more influence. He wrote with verve and realism about typical people of his time. He was an opinionated character. The man is a story all his own."

"Tell me about him."

"I have read Mathurin was a nephew of the poet Philippe Desportes and went to Rome with him until his immoral ways got him into trouble. The family stories say he returned to France under the protection of Desportes and became canon of Chartres." Peter's unflinching gaze into Elisa's eyes as he told the story, made her nervous. "Show me the farm, Peter."

"If you promise to call me Pete."

"Your parents call you Peter."

"Not always. They have this way of honoring my great grandfather, who I am named after."

"I think that is nice."

"I suppose. You call me Pete. Promise?"

"Yes, Pete."

Her answer gave Pete confidence. He took her hand and pointed towards the farm. "Lisa, do you see how the home is laid out with a purpose? The stable is to the north, against the woods for protection from winter's cold and the sleeping rooms face the south for light."

"That is wise."

"My dad does not know who in the family originally built it. Whenever someone married, they made extra changes."

"What changes?"

"Dad added a wall in the sleeping room, dividing it into two rooms. Few peasants have separate sleeping rooms. Our woods supply us with all the fuel and lumber we need. Let us go over here."

"I did not noticed this path. Where does it go?"

Pete guided her a bit further. "Let us sit down here awhile. I will tell you the story about this path." They found a soft, mossy patch of earth and sat, leaning against a large hickory tree.

"My grandfather had a problem of getting to church on time. He tired of the nagging it created and hewed a shortcut through the woods to the church. He did not want others to know his secret. He planted this hedge and underbrush to hide it. Otherwise, you must travel south on the Paris road past our garden and continue west two kilometers; take the first turnoff for one kilometer and turn left about one and a half kilometers in order to reach the church. As Pete spoke, he slowly slide his arm around Elisa. "Our church stands on the other side of our woods."

Elisa stood, took Pete's hand and pulled him forward. "Let's dance."

"Lee-e-e-sa, I can't dance."

"I will show you what my dad taught me." They danced the polonaise, circling, stepping, and promenading down the path until they reached the clearing. Their gleeful laughter stopped upon viewing the serenity of the scene. They looked steadily into each others eyes. Elisa was too bewildered to speak, and looked downward.

"If you will keep looking at me, I will tell you a fairy story." There was silence as they faced each other. Pete tried to make up a story to fit his feelings. "Once upon a time there was a girl and a boy upon a steep and dangerous mountain slope. They stood looking at each other, when a dream cloud fell from above. The engulfing dream made their world still, and bound them in its vacuum. Each harbored identical thoughts, asking themselves. Do I love this dream? Would I harm this dream? It was their moment the world stood still.

Pete squeezed her hand and looked at the scene before them. The peaceful sight was an anti-climax and calmed their beating pulses. Pete leaned over, wrapped his arms tightly around Elisa and fervently kissed her. "Will you marry me, Lisa?" She shyly lowered her head, twitched her sandal into the sod and answered, "Yes, my keeper of the path." They reached for each other's hand, stared at the clearing and pondered their new awakening.

Elisa shoved Pete and took off on a run back to his home. He quickly raced past her and shouted. "Viola. Viola." Abruptly, he stopped at the entrance to make a comical jump over the threshold. He had his parent's attention and plopped himself into a chair, breathless and panting. He rested back in the chair. "We shall marry."

"Where is Elisa?" Marie asked, still stunned by her son's juvenile antics. "I raced her down the path. Here she comes." He pulled a chair near him, "Sit here, Lisa." She sedately sat, looked at Pete's dad and said, "He is already, running away from me."

"I would think twice about the clown. What do you think, Marie?"

"I think we had better do some planning. Have you set a date?"

"Soon. Soon." Blurted Pete.

"Son, watch your manners. The wedding date is Elisa's choice." Elisa was not accustomed to warm attention and spoke hesitantly. "As soon as church bans can be announced."

"You have our blessings." Andy reached to shake Pete's hand. Maria hugged Elisa. "Elisa, you seem worried, is there a problem? You realize you will be living with us. Is that a problem?"

"Oh no, mame."

Pete grasped her folded hands from across the table and tenderly kissed them. "Dad, we are going to build another room."

"You bet. We can start felling trees from the east woods tomorrow."

"I have no dowry." Stammered Elisa, hiding tears with her cupped hands. Andy banged his fist upon the table. "Hell, we are not like those monarchs."

"Oh these men and their language." Marie went over and embraced Elisa. "Do not worry dear, I have collected many items in my chest over there, waiting for this moment when we would have a daughter."

"I have a stack of my stitchery." Said Diane. Elisa's tears continued, but flowed from joy and happiness.

"What about your mother? We could build another room." Asked Pete. Elisa shoke her head back and forth and dried her tears. "She never leaves the house. Has lived as a recluse since dad died and will never change. I will have to make checks on her."

"Peter you best leave and go share the good news with her mother." Said Andy.

"Elisa, let us have a cup of cidar first."

"The race did make me thirsty." Marie took a jug of cidar from the earthen pit and poured cups for all. "Come with me a minute, son." She led Peter into her sleeping room, opened a wooden-carved box and removed a ring. "This was my grandmother's ring. On your walk over to Elisa's, give it to her." Pete hugged his mother so tightly she squealed. Pete walked Elisa to her small shed-like hovel on the outskirts of Paris. Marie and Andy sat alone at the table, sipping cidar and relishing the good news. "Remember? You said you would pray for mother nature to run its course? I would say your prayer was quickly answered."

"Not any too soon."

"Why that is blasphemy, dear."

"It is a matter of months before he is liable to be conscripted." He closed his eyes in a quick, silent prayer.

"It has been awhile since you said anything about him turning eighteen."

"Why would I want to put a damper on his joy?"

"I know the war is still going on over there, but what have you heard about it?"

"I have talked to both Jacque and Phillip. Since last March, the village talk has not been good. The war in America is continuing, and Europe could get further involved." This shocked Marie and she found it difficult to simultaneously share the day's joy and the future's fear. She would move about. Get more cider. "Want another cup of cider?"

"Good idea." Andy spotted her anxiety. He knew how quickly she busied herself when worried, and decided to distract her thoughts. "Would you heat the cider?" Marie momentarily stiffened, realizing he did not drink hot cider in warm weather. When the hot cider was ready, Marie pulled a crock full of shelled chestnuts from the cabinet and placed a fistfull onto a plate. They munched and sipped. "What is this war about?"

Andy recalled how Peter had asked the same question, and repeated his same answer--"greed."

"I have gone over this before, dear."

"I know, but I can not seem to understand such suffering."

Andy said nothing, just munched on nuts and sipped his cidar. Diane put her cidar down with a thud. "Son, you become so aggravated and angry when you speak of war, your anger makes it difficult for us to think about what you are saying." Daniel nodded, "She is right, son. I know it is hardly fitting to speak of war in gentle terms, but it could help the women understand."

"I will try. Rivalry over whose to dominate Germany. Austria or Prussia? Rivalry over sea supremacy--our navy or Britain's? It has worsened from all the alliances that are forming. Austria, Russia, and Spain are with us, and on the other side is Prussia, Britain and

Hanover."

"Russia? She was not our ally in the War of Austrian Succession."

"No, she was not, Marie. Jacque was telling me, his nephew, who joined the stuffy Encyclopedists' group, said it was the Austrian, Count von Kaunitz, who managed to reverse European alliances of the war. Even Mme. de Pompadour put her influence into these alliance negotiations."

"We all know where her brains are."

"Why Marie, is your halo slipping?"

"Oh, it is such a worry."

"Marie, the elite, career-military are called first, before they call lowly, peasants. Another problem are the officers itching to distinquish their careers through battle after battle. But there is a small glimmer of hope."

"What? Tell me."

"Marie, give me a chance. Remember Peter's hero, Francois Quesnay? He leads a group of economists, whose theory is, the wealth of France lies in productive agriculture. Do not know how much influence his group has, but Quesnay was once the physician of Louis XV. We peasants could be forced to man our farms to feed the army. I would not get my hopes up. It is hard to make any sense out of these times."

Pete's singing became louder as he neared the door and entered. "I see you still have nuts from last fall? Where have you been hiding them?" He went over to the water bucket, dipped the tin cup and drank. "The walk made me thirsty."

"It is a short walk going and a long walk home, eh son?"

"Yes. I hate to think of Lisa walking to her mother's during the coming winter."

"Sit down Pete, and tell us how her mother took the good news?"

"Lisa told me more as we walked. She said her mother had attempted suicide twice. She tried to tell me not to expect any reaction from her mother, for she is in a world of her own. I figured she was exaggerating, so I was not prepared for the meeting.

Mom, you would not believe it. When we came in, she was sitting and weaving at her treadle. I shouted, 'We are getting married.' Her mother did not move. Did not look up. She continued footing and sliding the loom. Lisa walked to her mother, bent over with their noses almost touching, and told her we were getting married. Her mother's right hand continued working the loom, while her left hand pushed Lisa's face away. She said nothing. Just weaved, neither faster, nor slower. I followed Lisa's lead and sat down. We both related our plans to her mother. Dad, it was like talking to a wall."

"You were not talking to a wall, son. You have done your duty. Now, you will have a better understanding of Elisa and an insight into her unfortunate childhood. She is a dear child and one to cherish. Her mother is ill. I have seen many a widow of the wars become broken from heartbreak and loneliness."

Supper was usually the same each evening--bread and butter or milk and bread. Each bowed their heads for grace. One mind filled with joy and dreams. The other minds filled with anxieties.

"Peter, do not forget to snuff the candles before going to bed. Dad and I are tired. We will see you in the morning." Andy rose, picked up the paper he was sitting on, and turned to Pete. "A few days ago, I found this discarded Rambler at Josua's. Thought you might like to read it."

"Goodnight dad. I will snuff the candles."

Soon the extra room was built. To save time, the stone flooring was not continued. Instead, wooden planks were laid. Long ago the house had leant itself to several unique features. Most stable-areas were level with the living area, but not this one. In order for the stable to be adjacent to the north woods, it had been constructed on ground that dipped and then slanted upwards into the woods. Although the rooms were level, the dip made a dropoff on the northside, separating the stable from the hearth. Andy had put up a railing and replaced the rocks with steps leading down into the stable. When Andy married, he boarded up part of the stable railing for use as a root-cellar. In the past, there had been many times, wheat sheaves were stacked against the root-cellar, hiding foodstuff and fowls from ramsacking troops.

Completion of the room freed Pete to walk to Paris and work for Charles Antoine at his blacksmith and livery, where the wealthy boarded their carriage horses. His wedding plans needed money. There was not time to earn enough to buy a horse, but there was time to earn enough to take Lisa into Paris. Lisa had mentioned what a thrill it would be to hear six year old Wolfgang Mozart, who was on tour in Paris. Thoughts of his plans created such excuberance, he vaguely felt fatigued from his additional labor.

The existing hardship and despair were eased from the family's new found happiness over Pete's marriage. At eventide, with the day's work done, Andy began whittling parts for a cradle and wondered if his heir would be a son. Seldom during the war, had he the opportunity to indulge in dreamy thoughts and bliss of added family.

Last year had been another lean harvest with few wheat sheaves to prop into the stable. Andy finished making the cradle, his limp improved and he had his hickory cane carved in swirls and ornate designs. During Andy's leg recovery, Pete not only managed the farm and his work at the blacksmith, but also made walks to the village for papers and books. Diane, Marie and Elisa had completed a baby layette. Elisa wove blankets during the visits with her mother. The baby would soon be here. Andy mixed mud and straw and chaulked the house timbers.

"What are you doing, mom?"

"Found these rabbit hides drying on the stable wall. If I stitch them together you can tack them on the windows to keep out this dampness. It is affecting dad's leg. I can tell from the way he stays off of it. He has not walked to the village for several days. Hate to see this rain come with its chilly winds."

Elisa dipped candles for the coming spell of dark, gloomy days. Candles burned all day in the closed, dark interior. Pete glanced at Andy, whose nose was buried in a book. Papers and stacks of books surrounded his rocker. He kept abreast of many translated works of Gotthold Lessing. Andy's trips to borrow, but seldom buy, had caused villagers to nick-named him "the bouquiner," (hunter and collector of old books). Even at the parish library, the priest began calling him, "bouiquiner."

"Is the fire out? I feel a chill. Think I will take a nap." Said Marie. Peter put more logs on the fire and yanked his coat and hat from a wall-peg. "I am going to cut more logs." Andy sat his book aside, stood with cane in hand. "Let us do that, son. We will put the extra pile in the stable." Marie scornfully flopped her stitchery from her lap and onto the table with a snap, "Andy, there is sleet in this rain. I do not want you go out in this weather."

He stood erect. "Woman, do I tell you not to stitch with your crippled hands? Where are my mitts?" Andy never mislaid anything outside the house, but inside was different. His wraps were missing. He accused Marie of hiding them.

Pete gathered his crossbow and quivers, as ammo was used sparingly. "I am going to the east woods to scrounge up a hare for dinner. How are you feeling, Lisa?"

"Fine, dear. Baby's arrival is a few days off."

Andy shut his book, and smuggly muttered. "Do not worry, son.

I will warn you with a shot gun blast. When you hear that, you best, high-tail it home.

CHAPTER 5: ESSENCE OF LOYALTY

Monty had heard about sea-sickness, but never thought it could be so bad. The bread roll did ease his squimish stomach. Dizzily, he weaved towards the deck rail. Grasping the rail, he lingered in thoughts of the past as he slowly nibbled on his roll. Monty felt at a loss, with nothing to do but drift into his sea of memories. Monty's memory of Andy's life, was more vivid than those of past ancestors.

Elisa gave birth to Joseph Mark at dawn, according to Hoyle. She lay with her infant, feeling the rapture had to subside, or she would burst from joy. Andy was elated, but did not care to reveal too much delight. He would do as usual, relax in his rocker and read. Pretend to read while his thoughts evolved into fantasies of his grandson and things they would share. Marie glowed with pleasure, now that she faced new importance and responsibilities.

Pete felt lost in a mixture of emotion and conflict. He was overwhelmed with joy and awe, love and fear; and the responsibility of his newborn's destiny. Love made him too vunerable, opening his heart to possible pain. He felt a shiver that popped goose-bumps over his skin.

Andy had to make sure, "Pete, Elisa says he will be christened Joseph Mark. Is that your plan?"

"Sure is, dad. Our boy, Joseph Mark de Regnier."

Andy inhaled deeply. "That pleases me." Immediately Pete felt another new emotion. Was he now, someday, to be head of the family, replacing dad? There was no question about it. Pete had no answers and plenty of worries.

In the excitement, Diane and Daniel were not missed. Andy suddenly noticed. "Marie, dad and mom are not up yet. I am going to check on them. They will want to hear the good news."

Andy and Daniel came from the bedroom. Andy's arm was around Daniel as he slowly guided him to his rocker. "Marie, you better tend to mom. She is ill. Looks like the sweating sickness." Marie readied water, cloths, herbal balms, and hung a kettle of broth on the fire. She made checks on Elisa, but sat with Diane the rest of the day. Daniel was wrought with grief, worrying about Diane. In the evening, Andy retreated to his papers; papers served as an excuse to vent his anger from the anxiety over his mother. Andy felt alone in his emotions. Joy over his grandson, yet fear and grief over his mother. He lacked the patience to tolerate grief. "Continent's going to pot and he does nothing but play birds-and-bees. Fooled me. I thought he was a damn good statesman. Now I know better." In disgust, he tossed the Rambler into the fire.

"Now who has your goat?" Asked Pete.

"This is the fourth time the papers have written about the same dang doings."

"Are you mad at the paper?"

"I am. Also our foreign minister, Etienne Francois Duc de Choiseul. If he can not work at fixing an end to this war, why does he not work at fixing the conditions from it? No, the silly goof still busys himself with the marriage of six year old Marie Antoinette to Louis XVI. Toe-tipping around in his powdered wig and tight breeches, while our general, Louis Joseph de Montcalm was killed."

Pete grinned, he could see his dad's point, but thought he would change the subject. "The paper you tossed in the fire, you did not buy that paper. Where did you get that copy?" Andy did not expect the question. "Oh, round about. Find my papers at the village. It was on the counter at the fish market. I picked it up and walked out with it."

"You stole it?"

"If they wanted it, do you think they would have let me walk out with it?" Andy was easily irritated. His mother was ill and his dad was aging fast. He was caught in fate's bittersweet process of birth and death.

The sweating sickness killed Diane--Daniel's wife, Andy's mother, Peter's grandmere, and new-born, Joey's, great grandmere. She was buried in the cemetery by the church in the clearing where the path ends.

Andy hollered from the stable and interruped the women's work. "It is finished."

"I want to see." Said Elisa.

"Me too," Marie added, as both headed to the doorway.

Andy revelled in their praises. After his leg injury, during sedantary days and mourning, he had fashioned his own idea for a playcrib. One where Joey could crawl on the ground and still be enclosed by rails. In the springtime, he planned to stake it on the southeast side of the garden by the big oak tree. The women could work the garden while Joey played nearby.

"This is perfect. Joey will love it." Exclaimed Elisa. Marie enthusiastically spread her arms outwards, "What a blessing, Andy. Our garden work will fly by." Andy fiddled around with a crib corner appearing as though he was not delightfully absorbing every flattering word. He peered up, over, and around the crib corner. "This here is needing a bit more smoothing." As he worked, his mind conjured up another project. One he would think out. He would tell the women it was another root cellar. A cooler place during the heat of August. That would not be a lie. Yes, he could keep this plan secret and save the women useless worry. Andy was thankful his plan required more use from his hands, than from his legs.

Andy's rocker, like Daniel's and Pete's, was bordered with piles of reading material. However, Andy had Joey in his lap more often than a book. Andy rocked back and forth, pondering his plan while talking to Joey. "I am going to give you the best learning. We will keep reading. Everything I know, I will put into your adorable little head. You will be the best Attester, ever."

Marie bent over to Elisa and whispered, "Sure funny how Joey reacts so understandably." Andy overheard, "T'aint funny at all. He understands." Elisa reared back, letting out her squeal of infectious giggles which infected Marie's humor, and the duet of giggles ensued.

"Joey, you see how silly women can get? Best, they get back to their work. Your daddy is going to be in soon. Hungry as a bear."

When the women had gone to bed, Andy and Pete finished reviewing papers and were almost ready to retire. Pete snuffed the candles, when he heard a loud rumbling noise from the road. He relit a candle. "Dad, what do you suppose that is? Horses do not make that kind of noise."

"Let us take a peak. First snuff out that candle." Silhouetted in the moonlight were lines of soldiers, calvary, wagons and canons headed northwest along the Paris roadway that ran past the garden and the big oak tree.

"We have only had troops passing That is an army. What splendor." Said Peter. Andy cringed at his son's youthful awe and excitement over the Royal troops. "Do not like it, son. Let us go to the well. Want to talk with you." Pete seldom heard his dad's voice so dismal. Quietly, and obediently he followed, as Andy grabbed his cane and limped to the well. They sat upon the well's rim.

"When you were a child, did I use strength to overpower you?"

"No, dad. What is this about? Have I let you down?"

"No, just hear me out. Have I ever quarreled over whose the head

of this family or farm?"
"No."
"Have I denied your growing independence?"
"Not at all."
"Have I dominated you or stiffled your manhood?"
Pete bent over to cup himself a drink from the bucket, his answer echoed in the well, "Never, dad." Pete wondered if dad's health was failing along with grandpere's.
"I am glad to hear your answers. Hate to think I had indulged in oppressive, monarchial actions. Have I controlled your life?"
"Dad, of course, to some extent. You are the example I hold for myself."
"You are saying, I influence you?"
"Why, yes."
Andy smiled towards the heavens and sighed. He took a deep breath. Pete knew something was coming; something difficult for his dad to say. Andy paused, heaved a sigh, and took a deep breath. Pete waited for his dad to have his say. "Son, I can not control your life, but I can try to save it. You are seventeen and in a few months. . ."
'Dad, do not worry, the passing troops have not stopped. There have been no recuiters around."
Andy put his arm around Pete, "Do you want to wait until there are? Think of Elisa and Joey. And above all, consider your own beliefs. You have usually acknowledged my wisdom. You know I keep abreast of events and from what I have been reading it appears Britain's sea power will soon end this war. What I am trying to ask of you, son, is difficult. Should recruiters stop here, would you let me hide you in the root cellar? It is a matter of ideals, instead of this war's selfish, greedy, power goals of the monarchy." Remember the old story of Daniel's father who wept at the outbreak of the War of Polish Succession? He said back then, 'will war ever be fought for an ideal, a principal, instead of greed?'"
"Dad, I can not be a coward."
Andy took his arm from Pete's shoulder, "Son, what is your definition of a coward? Many are called coward, who are bravely stand up for their ideals. Ideals are far more dangerous and take far more courage. In the village of Marite, I know two families who sent sons away to Le Havre to hide in fish boats. The Loirets left with their three sons in a specially built wagon that hid them, and took the dangerous way south, to Argeles. Word got back, they are safely hidden in the Pyrennes.

You think about it. The cause that stirs a man's spirit should not be moved by a cause for greed--the greed of this monarch's regime. There is unrest in the colonies in America, and France has a sinister and foreboding unrest that could surface at anytime. I doubt if ending the war would, or could, change that. When you have come to your decision, let me know.

Now, let me tell you my secret plan. I do not want the women to know, yet. I am going to begin digging a hole in the west end of the root cellar."

"Back under the planking?"

"Yes. If the women get curious, it is to be a cooler spot during the summer for goat milk."

"Dad, you can not work like that."

"My arms have always been strong. I can sure as hell crawl and dig."

Pete's eyes widened in surprise, "Crawl? Where are you crawling?"

"Going to build a tunnel. The stable is next to the north woods. It will not be far to dig a tunnel to the underbrush by the path. Then, if need be, all of us can escape through the tunnel and hide in the church."

Pete stood up, then bent over in laughter, and slapped his dad on the shoulder. "That is a damn clever idea"

"Of course, I will have to tell the women when they begin to wonder why I am removing so much dirt. The first dirt, I will use to fill up the swine mud-holes in the stable. Then put the cart near the stable and empty dirt into it. I can handle a bucket, but will you do the dumping into the far west field?"

The women were now aware of the tunnel. It was July, and the heated earth had slowed the digging. The tunnel developed into an anticipated, forthcoming celebration upon its completion. Jocy's first birthday present was Rover, a black and white puppy. Onc, Pete had gotten from Jacque.

Andy sat down for breakfast and announced, "Made alot of progress yesterday. Should have the tunnel done before harvest." He looked around the room, "Mom, where is dad?" Marie did not look at Andy. She stirred her porridge. "Sleeping. He has been very tired of late." Pete finished drinking buttermilk from his Toby jug. The prized, birthday gift from his folks and Elisa. Toby imports were new. His was a Squire Toby, holding a tankard and pipe.

"Listen. Rover is barking. Barks are coming from the road."

Andy rose and entered the sleeping room to peer through the peak-hole. He hopped back as quickly as his cane allowed. "Troops, they are headed here. Pete get into the root cellar. You women clear the table."

Pete stepped down into the stable, crawled and squeezed himself into the small root cellar. Andy followed, grabbing stacked wheat sheaves and propping them along the length of the root cellar's siding. He brushed dust from his clothing and walked up the steps. He had prepared the family well. Elisa had cleared the sleeping room of Pete's clothing and was playing with Joey. Marie had cleared the table and began washing plates. His eyes scanned the room and spotted Pete's jacket hanging on the wall. He yanked it from the hook, opened a floor bin and dropped it into the earthen hole. With a flourish of his hand, pushed the dirt around the plank flooring until it appeared undisturbed. Andy had dug two floor pits, and built lids with stones set in mud to match the flooring. The women casually went about their work, as Andy answered the knock at the door. He opened only the upper-half. There stood a clean, uniformed officer with three soldiers.

"What can I do for you"

"Where are your sons?"

"We have but one son, commandant. He left last April for Paris. We do not know where he is."

"He joined there?"

"The day after his eighteenth birthday."

"We will look around." The officer reached over and unlatched the bottom-half of the door and entered with the soldiers. Marie hovered around the soldiers, "You must be tired, sit. I have made tarts for fall festival. You boys could use some buttermilk and repast."

Andy situated himself in his rocker. "Where are you boys, headed?"

"We have the area northwest of the Seine to census."

"Does that extend to Mayenne?"

"No, but up to Calais."

"That is over 200 kilometres." Andy added, sympathetically.

"Those are our orders. Orders to reach Calais by February."

"That is next to impossible. You are to cover all the extending areas?"

The officer swallowed his last bite of delicacy and shoke his head, "There are so many small villages, we willl probably end up over-looking many. You have quite a collection of papers over there.

Would appreciate any updating you could offer. We seldom have news."

Marie poured a refill of buttermilk into each soldiers' cup. One soldier looked up over his shoulder into her face, "Just like my mom, trying to fatten me up." Marie stroked his shoulder lovingly and knew how his mother must miss him. Concern for these soldiers tore at her heart. Were these young French boys destined to return? She battled to repress the fostering guilt of hiding her son.

"Marie, how about refilling my cup, too?" Andy's remark brought laughter from the soldiers. "Harvest has allowed little time for reading, but read where Charles Messier, one of our leading astronomers, published his catalogue listing 109 newly discovered celestial objects."

A soldier turned to the Commandant, "We should have that book, maybe it could help us at night. We have to use the stars for direction, especially in these heavily forested areas."

Marie excused herself, "Must see how Elisa and the baby are doing. I shall pray every star leads you boys safely home." Andy noticed the hanky she quickly pulled from her apron pocket as she left. He smiled at the soldiers, "You will excuse mom. Our women get rather emotional over this war."

There were no smiles upon the soldiers' faces, but each nostalgically nodded their heads. The officer suddenly snapped his soldiers to attention. "Must get back to my troop in the road."

The soldiers had brought into the room their charm of youth and innocence, and went with them when they left. Gone so quickly, it left a void in the room. Andy did not move for awhile. He, like Marie, felt heartache. Why should these polite, disciplined, obedient French youths be manipulated into a false sense and cause of loyalty to risk their lives, only for monarchial greed? Andy stepped into the stable, removed the sheaves and Pete crawled out. "Long stay, dad."

"Yes. All went well, this time."

"Dad, I still feel . . . "

"Never mind Pete. You ponder further on the matter of loyalty. It was obvious these boys had not been in battle, fresh, wet-behind-the-ears, misguided patriots. If they live through battle, they will reflect and question whether their loyalty was an honest French cause, or whether their loyalty had been misused as a tool for monarchial greed and power.

Son, the next time troops show, you could be out in the field. You will have to quickly take cover. Get to the woods fast, and head for the tunnel. Drop whatever you are doing. It will appear as though I left my field work to come in for a rest. Understand?"

Pete did not answer. Unprepared and undecisive, he had followed his dad's order to hide. Hiding left him feeling uncomfortable, in a state of limb; and understanding both a right and a wrong to his hiding.

Nature's growth stirred, hidden beneath the earth. The approaching springtime aroused family's spirits from their dormant, snowbound confines. Andy's ideas were sprouting into plans for upcoming activities. There was an air of excitement in Elisa speech. A higher tone in Marie's melodic voice. Pete's rambunctious teasing increased. Little Joey was not immune. Joy infected his being and stimulated his curiousity.

"Pete, there he goes. Lay the chair across the steps." Elisa had to constantly keep her eyes on Joey.

"Peers to me, he is going to be as high-strung as his dad." Marie chuckled. Pete stuck both hands in his pockets, reared back and boasted, "Now, that is a good omen." Elisa tugged at mom's apron and coyly dropped her head, "It was Pete's shyness that first caught my eye." Marie and Elisa embraced, leaned upon each other for support, and burst into convulsive laughter.

Andy's thoughts had been interrupted. "Pete, where is the bottle of spring tonic? The only sign I see, is women needing a dosage. Better make it a couple doses." In his rocker he made a pretense of reading, but was reviewing winter's passing. There had been no further military incidents. The tunnel was finished in time to be lined with rocks before the rains. Neither the past fall, nor spring rains had were the normal amount of rain; it followed the harvest would be poor. Plans must be made to compensate. A plan he would share with his neighbors for their benefit, as well as his own. He would discuss it with the family after supper.

There had been little entertainment. Village fairs and social gatherings stopped when war began. Eager for entertainment the women dwelled, weeks in advance, on birthday plans for Pete and Joey.

Pete hung his jacket on a peg. "Can not get used to these longer days." He walked to Elisa and squeezed her tenderly, "Joey sleeping?" Elisa nodded. Pete moved towards dad and sat. "Cleared that rocky corner in the field. Earth is softened and rocks lifted easily." Andy was delighted the back-breaking task was done. One, he had not wanted to ask of Pete. "Felt we have been plowing around those rocks long enough, and it will give us a bit more land."

"Where did you put those rocks?

"Piled them against the stable to add to the windbreak. Something wrong with that, dad?"

"The tunnel? Do you suppose it caved in?"

"No, I checked. Sturdy as ever. The rock pile blends in well with the terrain."

Marie placed a tureen of hot potato soup on the table. "Time to eat."

"Let us discuss the possibility of another poor harvest. I have a plan, but first there are problems and want your input. I also want to let our neighbors in on the plan. Which brings up the problem. How do we get our work done, and still spread this plan around? The talk in the village has been about troop wagons pillaging the area southwest of Paris, and even going into Vendee. The army's desperate need for foodstuffs will only worsen with the troop movements spreading north. Except for a few occasions, this area has been left alone because of the small acreage of each farm and the abundance of woodlands. A poor harvest will wreck havoc."

"Dad, what is your plan?"

Andy reached for his ink and quill as Elisa bent over and picked up the blank paper resting on the nearby stack of books. "Interrupt me if you have ideas. First, we should not do as always. We will not plant all of our harvest grain. The harvest seed will be divided into two parts--part one and part two.

From part I, we hide half of it. The other half, divide it too; with a fourth held for next year's seed and the other fourth, we store. From part II, we save half for next year's seed, and from its second half, we plant two-thirds in our field. We plant one-third in the woods, which can not be seen by passing troops."

The family had a new adventure. Their excitement increased, as each listened attentively. "Mind you, we will not clear the woods for it, just sow it among open, scattered spaces within the woods. After it matures, we can easily spot it. It will take more work and time to reap. We will also, divide the garden and put part of it in the woods. Another project is Joey's play-crib that he has outgrown. I will remove it for more garden space. Our field and garden may not produce well, but the woodland plantings should do well in the moist and shaded woods."

"We can not lose from the plan. Without it, we could lose alot, and especially since troop wagons are taking more and more." Said Marie.

"What is next?" Pete asked.

"I will pen the plans on this sheet. We will need several copies." Said Andy.

"I can do that." Said Elisa.

"Once that is done, we need to figure out how to get the plan safely to our neighbors. The plan could prove dangerous, if it was in the wrong hands. It would be obvious to taille collectors, purveyors, and the king's military, and would be decreed a criminal act of treason, punishable by execution. This plan subjects us and our neighbors to risk." Except for Andy, everyone's adventurous mood had changed. The air of adventure was gone.

"Marie, would you get us some hot tea?"

"I will, dad." Elisa jumped to the task.

"Maybe, we should forget this plan." Said Andy.

"I am not going to let my family starve. I know that much." Said Pete. Elisa turned around with the boiling tea kettle in hand, "I can not bear to think of Joey crying for food."

"Dad, what about you? Asked Andy. "Like it. Sounds like woodland planting is one chore I would be able to do."

"How do you feel about it, Maria?" She shifted around in her chair, thinking for a moment before answering, "Starvation or death, is there a difference? In these risky times, people are being arrested and executed for doing nothing. You men will have to decide."

Andy picked up the pen. "Guess, we go ahead with the plan. We are back at the problem of distributing it. Any ideas? You know we will be twice as busy planting in both areas. Can not see how we will have time to reach neighbors, who will also be in their busiest season."

"What about a Sunday afternoon meeting?"

Pete, it is definitely too risky. Police are under orders to report all gatherings and assemblies. Villagers still talk, in hushed tones, about the Touraine incident."

"What was that about? Asked Marie.

Andy scratched his beard, delaying a moment to decide if he should tell the women. "It was over a year ago. The entire Michelet family, a large family that had scattered into Orleanais, Marche, Maine and Poitou, decided to meet for a day of picnicking at Touraine. They were all arrested and investigated for days, before being allowed to return home. Their stories about imprisonment and the prisoners they saw were atrocious."

"Why didn't you tell me about it?"

"Haven't you enough worries?"

"Could we leave copies in the church?" Asked Elisa.

"No. Absolutely not. We do not need to place the church in danger. Under different circumstances, that would be an excellent idea." Said Marie.

"If we do not share the plan with neighbors, it will not put them in danger." Said Pete. Elisa looked at Pete in astonishment, then turned to speak to Andy. "I could not eat if I knew Jacque's family was hungry." Andy reached towards Elisa and lovingly pinched her chin, "You are so right." Elisa basked from Andy's favor, and gloried in her ability to out-shine one of Pete's remarks. Pete yawned and said, "I am tired. It is getting late. We do not seem to be getting any place with this problem." Andy rose, and snuffed the candle. "We will discuss it tomorrow, after we have had time to think about it."

At breakfast, Marie banged a wooden mallet on the table as she gleefully announced, "I have found the answer. You men complicate things. There is a simple answer."

"Let us hear it woman. In a few simple words." He bent his head, trying to hide his smile. Marie paused, she wanted to gain everyone's ear, "Elisa and Joe can hunt for fresh grouse and pheasant eggs in the woods to add to what my hens lay. I shall take two baskets of assorted eggs around to neighbors, while you men tend to planting."

"No one has money to buy eggs. Farmers still have a few hens. How does that help our plan?" Asked Pete.

"As I was saying, there will be no risky, written plan. I will explain the plan and its risks to each neighbor. Give them some eggs, so as to empty my basket. Along the way, if I am stopped on the road and quizzed, will say I am a simple peasant trying to sell eggs." Andy reached across the table to clutch her hands and gaze into her face, saying, "My egg-lady has hatched the answer."

"Marie, dangers lurk all over France, but none as absurd as what I read yesterday." Said Andy.

Pete winked at Marie and asked, "The Rambler, again?"

"Yes. It was in the Rambler. What difference does that make? This French Huguenot, Jean Calas was tried and executed. He was accused of murdering his own son so his son would not become a Roman Catholic. He protested his innocence, but to no avail. Ever hear anything so bizarre and disgusting?"

"What if he was guilty?" Asked Pete?

"Guilty? Then it would be another example where religious loyalty existed as a poison, instead of a faith." Andy's anger subsided, he mumbled to himself. "Dangers . . . Danger everywhere."

It had been a long time since the joy of birthday celebrations and the fall festivals had lightened fatigued bodies and worried minds. Pete turned nineteen in 1762, and soon after, Joey reached two years. Andy had whittled a boat for Joey's birthday. The boat took precedence over Rover, who previously occupied Joey's playtime. The boat also took over the goat's drinking trough. Joey would squat on the floor and pushed the boat back and forth the length of the trough.

"Where is your boat going? Asked Andy.

"Merica."

"Joey, what did you say? Asked Pete.

"Merica."

Marie placed both hands on her hips, scowled at Andy and said, "There. You see what your opinions have been doing? Is that what you want to teach your grandson? Go to America. You had better watch what you discuss when he is around."

"Marie, your question is conditional. Depending upon conditions here, and conditions on where one is going. Right now, Catherine the Great is inviting Germans, for this year and next, to Russia. She is not giving them land, but promises no taille for thirty years."

"It would take a strange German to trust Catherine II." Said Marie.

Elisa felt the need to interrupt. "Dad, would you begin teaching Joe about time and the calendar?

"Yes, Joey should be learning how the months roll by."

With each month's passing, the land became drier and drier. The plantings in the woods flourished. In August, the parched garden and field were quickly gleaned of its scant fruits. Harvesting in the woods was anxiously awaited, and no one was annoyed by its tedious reaping. Even Rover dug up potatoes, while Joey gleefully picked them up and dropped them into a basket.

France's annual celebration of fall festivals were again cancelled due to war and drought. Andy's planting-plan had worked. The field harvest was sparce, but the woods yielded more than expected. The grateful gleaners and neighbors held their own festivity within their hovels.

"Dad, I sacked the planting grain for next year and put it in the root cellar. The cellar is not going to hold everything. Should we make another root cellar?" Asked Pete.

"I have been thinking about it. Might dig a small one in the stable under the steps. Can not use the woods, everything would sprout or spoil. If we can not store all of our harvest, my plan is a bust."

"No dad. We can figure out a way. With all our wood, could we put in a false ceiling? It would hold alot. We could even hang stuff from the rafters."

"That is an idea, son. Let me think it out. The ceiling could not be more than two feet from the rafters and with no inside entrance. Inside, it can not have any obvious opening or appear as though there was enough room for someone to hide. We could disguise an opening outside, that could be reached only with a ladder. It is possible. That is a terrific plan, Pete. Let us get started on it tomorrow."

Trees were felled, sawed, and carefully placed inside the stable. As each ceiling plank was laid, the women handed harvested bundles to the men, who arranged them in the new storage area. Andy gathered everyone around him, pointing his finger at one, and then the other. "I do not want anyone leaving the stable ladder leaning against the outside, or making daily use of this storage. It can easily be spotted by passing troops and arouse curiosity. We will still need to make another root cellar under the stable steps for daily usage. I will attach the steps to a pull-rope for easy opening. Should troops or ruffians arrive to raid our root cellar, it will be the only cellar we show them."

There was no rain until November. Then came frost and sleet. Andy huddled near the fire. "Weather has been a repeat of last year. France is in a terrible famine. Might have to repeat our planting plan next spring."

"We are all trained to it now, dad. Should not be a problem."

Elisa walked over to Pete, guiding Joey with one hand, "Feel how warm he is." Pete picked Joey up and felt his forehead, "He does not have the sweats, does he?"

"That is what I thought at first. I have been watching him for three hours and finally figured it out. It is the new ceiling. It keeps the floor much warmer." Marie felt her forehead, "You know, I have noticed that, so different than last winter." Andy stopped staring into the fire and turned to Marie, "Bet cha' thought you were getting the sweating sickness, eh?"

Elisa's mother died suddenly from natural causes. Elisa had spent many hours sitting by her silent mother as she weaved her endless swaths of cloth. She would arrive to see her mother amidst fold-after-fold from her on-going weaving. Elisa would scoot her mute mother aside and briefly take over the loom to close the endless weaving.

Elisa never succeeded in her quest to break her mother's silence. There were three gifts her mother left her: the loom, weaving skill, and piles of woven material. Elisa and Marie decided to use the material to cover and replace the straw bed-layers. They had struggled with the bundling of flax and straw, interlaced until they had constructed mats for each bed.

"No. No, Joey. Stay out of the sack."

"Oh, Elisa, let him play with a few more feathers."

"Now, mom. He will want a feather, then another and another. You would not care if he scattered feathers everywhere. Now would you?"

"Joey, want grandmere to make you some applesauce? There are apples in the root cellar."

"No, gamma. Wan 'ta nuth-a feth-ur,"

"You were right, Elisa. He is after more feathers. I should get busy with the pillows. My geese do give good batches of down."

"Yes, they are dandy ganders, Mom." Marie knotted a thread and tossed the pillow. "We are almost finished. Merci, we will sleep so snuggly, we will not be able to get up." Marie, dreamily looked up into space as she said, "In a few years, there might be enough goose-down to replace the flax with feathers." Elisa nudged Marie. "Dad probably would not sleep on them, figuring it a luxury of monarchist influence." Marie and Elisa's laughter filled the room and Joey thought they were laughing at him and his goose feathers.

"Me funny?" Joey giggled.

CHAPTER 6: THE PURVEYOR

"You call this lunch? Water and bread?"

"You need not eat it." The captain passed on to the next hungry person.

Monty could not eat, and kept his roll for later. His stomach was turning and he pulled out some paraffin to chew. Everywhere he looked, people were vomiting. The children were not as ill as the adults. A whalefish came alongside and did flip-flops. Flip-flops like my wheezy stomach, thought Monty. Again, in hopes of stopping his dizzy, whirling sensation. He struggled for memories to distract him from nausea. He remembered a story about a perveyor.

Andy's plan ran smoothly. It was no longer a tense subject of after-dinner conversation. Outside, the rain continued a steady downpour.

"More salt-pork and beans." Said Andy.

"And bread." Pete gestured, pointing to the bread basket.

"You men worked up an appetite." Marie walked to the fire and loaded the plates from the black, hanging pot. Andy glanced at Joey. "Would you look at that. Joey's fallen asleep." Pete reached over and felt Joey's forehead. Elisa, rose from the table and carried Joey to bed. "Do not worry, Pete. All day he was blowing and chasing falling goose feathers. He is worn out."

"Now, that Elisa is gone, isn't her birthday soon? What do you think of surprising her with a silhouette of Joey? They are the rage around Paris. Started from the black and white cut-outs made in the past by our finance minister, Etienne de Silhouette." Asked Andy.

"That is a wonderful idea. But I am sure I could not get Joey to sit still that long. Since he does everything his grandpere asks of him, you best do it." Said Marie.

"Fine. We will have to concoct a way to get Elisa out of the house."

"I can manage that."

Elisa returned. "Did I miss anything? What are you talking about?"

"This mess in Russia. Catherine the Great, I mean the mighty Empress of Russia, fan-dangled around to get her husband . . ."

"You mean Emperor Peter III? No one liked him. I remember as a boy, villagers teased me, asking if he was my namesake."

"As I was saying . . . , fan-dangled around to get her husband murdered in order to gain the throne. Wonder what gets into these women?" Between bites of food, Pete answered, "Damned if I know." Marie and Elisa's mouths twitched, but both managed to restrain giggles.

There was a knock on the door, a louder knock and then banging. "Who could that be at night? Pete, get into the cellar." The women rushed to clear everything. After stacking wheat sheaves against the root cellar, Andy rushed to the door. It was peg-leg Jacque, who would not be walking through the mud for idle chatter.

"What is wrong?" Asked Andy.

"Take those wet things off. Here, let me take and dry them." Elisa grabbed a pail near the door. "Put your peg-leg in here. I will get a knife to scrape the mud off. We have wrapping hides for it. Otherwise, by the time you walk home your wooden peg will be so wet, it could warp."

"Merci." Said Jacque as he bent over, talked and scrapped. "News is, everyone is uptight about a purveyor; and passing words of caution for fear one of us might let out our secret-plantings in our woodlands. Just one slip and we would all be caught."

"That is for sure." Pete casually sauntered up the stable steps. He had heard, and recognized Jacque's voice.

"You are liable to catch the sweating sickness, Jacque." Said Daniel.

"I figured at night, no one would see or stop me on the road. Felt this news should spread. Pete you will carry it north?" Pete nodded his head. Marie poured hot tea as the men gathered around the table. By now, Jacque had caught his breath and relaxed. "A purveyor is going through. He stopped at my place this afternoon, just at sunset. Said he would continue tomorrow. He bedded at the village inn." Andy leaned towards Jacque's bad ear. "Was there any trouble?"

"Trouble?"

"Yes trouble. Did he cause you any trouble?"

"No."

"Could you pay your taille?" Jacque slapped Pete's shoulder, "Yes, thanks to Andy's plan. Was a might short. Paid what I could and he settled for two bags of grain. That purveyor was a talkative one and sez we are in for some misery. Sez our army is being devastated, and in America, New France is no more."

"Oh, no." Sighed Marie as she braced herself against a nearby armoire.

"Go on, Jacque."

"What?"

"I said, go on, Jacque."

"The purveyor sez military wagons would be in this area seeking foodstuffs. They have already covered southern France. Plan to use taille records in order to find out who has the larger farms and what is owed."

"Never thought I would be saying I am thankful our farm is small." Jacque nodded in agreement. "Yes. You have only one field and the rest is woods. They may not even stop here. Better not count on it. Have you any people in Correze?"

"Have you, Marie?"

"No." She snipped.

"No, most of our relatives are in Champagne and Lorraine areas. Why?"

Jacque bent his head, gritted his teeth before beginning. "Taxer told horror stories about the south, especially around Correze. Sez there is terrible famine and growing pestilence. Forget how many he sez died from cholera, typhus and sweating sickness. Even deaths from rat bites. Rats so bad, farmers could not keep what little grain they salvaged. It is bad, real bad. Sez it will spread north in time."

"They do not have any dogs or cats to kill the vermine?"

"Pete, for years there has not been a cat or dog loose in the streets of Paris, and suppose it is the same in the southern area."

"Why?"

"People have eaten them. This is why rats have multiplied into this sorry state. Gotta' go now. Pete, you will pass the news on?"

"Sure will. Thanks Jacque."

"Sorry, bringing words so grim." Jacque hobbled off.

"What will we do?" Andy did not spend time discussing Jacque's news or answering Marie. His mind concentrated on their projected planning.

"Pete, you will have to stay in the house for the next few days. Dad and I will tend to the chores. Marie and Elisa will do the garden draining. The first person, entering this house, will be your cue to head for the hidden root cellar. You may not feel right about hiding; but you are not wrong either. Understand?"

"Lisa, could you handle both gardens alone for an afternoon?"

"I think so, Joey is minding better. He stays nearby, playing with Rover."

"Pete why does she have to do that?"

"Mom, I was wondering if you would mind walking to Jacque's and taking a couple of his dog's litter off his hands?"

"We have Rover to feed. You want two more dogs to feed?"

"Yes. Filthy, diseased rats are not going to get the upper-hand around here. These dogs will not be in the house. If food gets scarce, they can feed themselves from hunts in the woods. I am going to sketch plans for building some traps." Pete had an aversion to rats, an obsession of hatred since reading an article about the pestilence created by vermine, and how rats had gotten under the tall, full-bottomed wigs of the elite and bitten their scalps.

"Good thinking, son." Andy scanned the book stacks, selected a book and relaxed in his rocker. Marie began stacking plates. "Marie, make sure one of those pups is a female." She huffed around the table, until finally speaking her mind. "Good grief. We will have a herd of mongrels in no time."

At dawn, Pete walked north to pass the news to Gautier's. The rain had stopped and left a heavy mist. Later, he heard his mom's call, as she rattled the door. Marie shifted two puppies over to her left arm to open the door. She started to enter, when she noticed a man on a horse, pulling a cart towards the house. The horse trotted through puddles and passed the garden where Elisa and Joey were digging trenches. A gust of wind blew the flap of Marie's bonnet across her face. She brushed it aside and stared. He was not a soldier. His dress was similar to a gendarme with triangular hat and brim dipped in the center. He wore a belted coat to the knees with wide cuffs. He had no boots, but leggings with buckles that glistened even in the day's cloudy overcast.

"Pete, hide. Man on horse." Pete grabbed his whittling, brushed the shavings from the table and clamored down the stable steps. Marie ran to the sleeping room's peek-hole to further view the man. He was not in a hurry, but intently looked to one side and to the other. Marie walked back to the hearth thinking, he is gawking around, trying to measure the farm. She knew Elisa would bring Andy in, if he had not already seen the man. She would have until then, to handle the matter alone. There was a gentle knock on the door. Marie opened only the upper-half of the door.

"I am Bertrand Daubenton, taille collector in the service of his majesty. May I come in?"

"Have a seat."

"Where is your husband?"

"He is in the field. If he saw you ride up, he will be in soon. He walks slowly, due to his wounded leg."

"Oh, then I will spread these papers on the table and begin recording. What is your name and your husband's?"

"Marie and Lambert Andre de Regnier."

"You and your husband live here?"

"Yes. We also have a daughter and a grandson."

"Yes. I saw them as I rode up. Where is her husband?"

"Our son left a year ago, after his eighteenth birthday."

"That is the usual report on my travels. War takes them, while the farms are left for the old to manage. Makes the taille difficult to collect."

Andy entered the house. "You might want to help Elisa. I will speak with this man."

"Yes. Elisa could use an extra pair of hands." Marie was happy to be free of the pretentious man.

"I see you are here for the taille. How much do we owe?"

"First, there are some questions to ask." He looked down at Andy's leg. "War injury?"

"Yes, with the troops."

"Do not want to talk about it, eh? I run into the same thing with all you old-timers. I too, am doing my duty. Served His Majestery neer on ten years. You have one field and a garden?"

"Yes." The man dipped his quill into a small ink vial.

"What is your livestock?"

"There is ol' Ox, Bossie the cow, a goat, four sheep, three swine, and fowls."

"You have no horse?"

"No. Who can afford a horse?" Andy waited as the man scrib bled.

"The taille has been raised from last year." Andy rose to his feet and snorted. "Raised the taille, again? Could barely pay last year's."

"Sorry. What with the war and famine."

"Taille does not ease famine. We have to eat to raise grain." Said Andy in a huff and the man stiffened.

"I have no answers. I must collect."

"We have not quite saved enough. Poor harvest, you know." Andy went to a drawer, pulled out a draw-string bag and handed him the bag of savings. The man spread the year's savings over the table, counting and recording. "It is almost all there. Would you take some grain or chickens for the remainder?" Andy asked. The man rose from the table saying, "I do not know. Let me see your root cellar." Andy took his cane and hobbled towards the steps.

"Over here." Andy yanked on the rope and the steps rose.

"Never saw a gadget like that." He searched through the contents of the cellar. "Ah, see you have a jug of cidar, some potatoes. Any grain?"

"Two bags over there. We have to have grain for planting."

The man scratched his head. "Sack these potatoes. I will take them, the cidar, and a bag of grain. That should cover the taille."

Andy lowered the steps and the man walked back to the table and his records. He sat, jotting more details. He shuffled papers and put them and his ink into a leather satchel; tossed it over his shoulder saying, "Hope these potatoes do not get wet. Quickly, he picked up the jug and cradled it lovingly in his left arm. His right hand grabbed the sack and drug it behind as Andy opened the door, then shut and latched it. Andy listened and heard the plop of the grain bag hit the floor of the cart. He thought, the oaf probably burst the bag. He heard the snap of the reins as the cart pulled away. Andy shook his head in exasperation, betting the cidar would be gone within a kilometer.

"That man's sense of duty is akin to rock soup." Andy muttered to himself and walked to the stable steps to holler, "All clear." Pete appeared, he saluted his dad. "Dad, this proves what a fix the family would be in, had we not followed your plan." Pete went directly to the door, opened it and looked towards the garden. "I am going after Lisa and Joey. If they stay out much longer, they will get sick."

"Well, dear. How did it go?"

"He settled for a bag of grain, the cidar and all the potatoes in the cellar."

"All my potatoes? Glad we have more in the other storage. Joey's growing so. He thrives on those potatoes."

"Stop the gabbing and get out of those wet clothes." Said Andy.

"Here is our little mud-ball." Pete gingerly led Joey to the fireplace and began stripping him. Elisa had gone into a sleeping room to change her dress and returned to a room full of laughter. "What is so funny?" Marie cupped her hands over her mouth to stiffle laughter as she sputtered. "Look at Joey." His small, nude body danced and pranced in front of the fire's flashing lights as he tried to heat every curve of his cherubim body.

All sat, contentedly, after finishing the evening meal. Elisa asked, "Why so quiet? There is not any news items in the Rambler to cuss?"

"Let me see. Oh yes." He glanced and winked at Marie and Pete. They yelled in unison, "Happy birthday, Elisa." Marie jumped up and returned with a torte she made with dried berries plumped into juicy freshness.

Elisa gasped between sobs, "I am so happy. Love you so much."

Joey's fat cheeks shifted as he spoke each word, "Luvf ou, too. Mommie."

Pete reached for a box under his chair and sat it on the table. "Lisa, here is your birthday present from all of us. Even the wrapping is from all of us." Pete said, pointing to the center, "These are from some of mom's pressed flowers. The paper is one of dad's Rambler's. And the ribbon, well, I bought that for your beautiful hair."

"My ball. My ball, daddy."

"Oh, pardon me. Joey made this pretty, perfectly shaped mud-ball in the center of mom's flowers, and dried it by our fireplace."

"Mommie, open da' giff. Open."

"First, I want to save this beautiful mud-ball. Thank you, Joey." She carefully removed the wrappings to save each part. There lay the gift, a beautifully carved-framed silhouette.

"Me-e-e, mommie. It is me." Joey beamed in sheer delight and so elated, he forgot his other gift.

"Joey, you have something else for your mother?" Joey squealed as he remembered, and stood erect in front of Elisa and babbled. "Oui, Mommie. Heeb-oo-rarie."

"No Joey. Start at the beginning. Just as we learned." Joey quieted at Daniel's voice, and watched until he had everyone's attention. "Han-you-ary, Hee-boo-ary, Maa-sh, A-pill, May, Hoon, Hoo-lie, Aah-cust, Auch-toe-bah, No-mem-bah, Dee-sem-bah." Everyone clapped saying, "Wonderful. Wonderful."

CHAPTER 7: THE TUNNEL

Monty was still sick. People came from steerage for the supper of water, milk and bread, and returned below; too weak to weather the rocking deck. He stayed on deck as long as he could before all those above-board were ordered below and the steerage door locked. Monty found no sitting room on the crates and people were jammed together in the darkness. He did not want to sit in the putrid water that soaked his shoes. Like the others, he stood supported by the packed bodies until someone crumpled from exhaustion into the foul water. There was no alternative but to eliminate oneself, where one stood. The pit reeked of sewage, sweat, and tears. The smell of garlic added its rancid aroma.

Monty heard prayers mumbled in many languages which filled the night with a strange, dismal, pleading sound. He bent his head, shut his eyes and tried to sleep. The smell kept him awake. Never had he endured such indignities. Then he thought of the slaves that were transported in chains and gave a prayer of gratitude. Memories had been on his mind all day, and continued to take shape in his dreams. The pit had put fear on his mind; and fears of the old tunnel entered his dreams.

Springtime was late in 1763, and brought a dry summer and danger. Andy had finished the carved puppet for Joey's birthday. Marie's flock of fowls had increased. The open land withered from the sun's relentless heat waves; but the shaded woods teemed with flowers, birds and animals. As the summer lengthened, even the woods suffered from the intense heat.

In mid-afternoon Pete paused to rest. Would his hoeing benefit this drying field? He leaned on the hoe to rest, and heard a raucous from the woods. He dropped his hoe and ran into the woods, deeper and deeper into the forested terrain. He ran to the edge of his dad's wooded land. The noise was louder and came from a section of the Paris road which cut through woods and made a turn past the house.

Pete hid behind bushes to watch. Instantly, he realized these troops were returning from battle in need of food and re-enforcements. Some marched and others limped from wounds. The scraggly, torn and dirty uniforms showed more bandages than uniforms. Many were drunk and swinging jugs. Behind their scattered lines were wagons filled with the wounded and dying. The shouts, laughter, and groans lessened as Pete ran to the tunnel entrance.

"Dad. Get everyone into the tunnel. Drunken troops returning from battle up north, as their uniforms are caked with dried mud. Only the northern coast had rain during this drought."

The men dashed up the steps from the stable and into the room. "Troops coming. Into the tunnel. You first, Marie. Then Elisa and Joey. Then grandpere. Dad, you follow."

"No." Answered Andy.

"Do as I ask, dad. I want to make sure the tunnel entrance is well-hidden. Hurry. No time to argue."

Andy grabbed his cane and took his knife; bent over and cut a piece from the slab of dried meat hanging on the cellar's wall.

"Do not push." Complained Marie, as Andy tried to help her crawl into the tunnel.

"Well, put a little speed into it." Said Andy, and handed Elisa the piece of jerky. "Give this to Joey. Chewing on it will keep him quiet."

At the tunnel entrance, Joey took off in a bug-crawl. Pete waited a few minutes, knowing his dad would be slow to crawl while dragging his lame leg. Pete entered the root cellar and replaced its planked siding, while he shifted the bundled wheat sheaves back into a position. At tunnel's end, he replaced the disguised lid and walked onto the path. The others were down the path, and he ran to catch them. The family safely reached the church.

"Pete, when do you think we can return?"

"They are drunk, mom. Probably pass-out and sleep the night. Reckon they will not pull out until noon. I will find Father Moreau and ask if we can spend the night in the basement."

Father Moreau shared supper with the family. "You better not leave until dusk tomorrow."

The next evening, the family walked the path homeward, but stopped at the edge of the woods. "You stay here until I wave to you with a candle." Said Andy.

"Wagons are gone. I do not see anyone."

"Pete, you stay with the family. Could be sleeping it off in the house. A hobbling, old man returning home will not alarm them." Pete watched until Andy reached the house. He did not come out as expected. Pete told the family to move further back into the woods.

"We can not see from back here." Complained Marie.

"Nevermind. I am watching." Pete could not stand the wait any longer. He feared Andy was in trouble. He walked back to the women. "Grandpere, you make sure everyone stays right here. Do not move from this spot. Mom, after I enter the tunnel, see that the edges of the tunnel lid are well-brushed."

"Something is wrong, I know it." Marie moaned.

Andy entered the house, gropped his way to a chest drawer that held Elisa's candles. The candlelight revealed a grotesque scene. The house was in shambles. A burning pain shot through his arm and tightened around his chest, holding him motionless. Dazed, he lost track of time. He viewed their broken possessions in a daze, and waited for the pain to subside.

Pete crawled out of the tunnel and stealthily entered the stable. Hearing nothing, he grabbed the hay-hook from the wall. He sneaked and peeked around the corner. Andy was standing alone in the middle of the wreckage, slowly viewing the debris.

Pete entered and threw the hay-hook to the floor. "Why didn't you wave us in? You worried us all." Startled, Andy looked at Pete in puzzled surprise and stammered, "Sorry. I got carried away viewing this pillage." Andy's face was shallow, wane, and sweaty. "Dad, you are ill." Pete glanced around seeking a chair not broken; yanked it towards himself and guided Andy into it. He ran to the sink, soaked a cloth in the water bucket and put the wet cloth upon Andy's forehead.

"I am feeling all right now, son. Whatever it was, it is gone. Do not tell the women."

Pete stood in front of Andy and put both hands upon his dad's shoulders. "I will not say anything, if you stay put in the chair until I get back. In this darkness the women may not see me wave. I had them go further back into the woods. Are you sure you are all right?"

"Sure, go get our family."

The tedious crawl through the tunnel had been too much strain for Andy. Pete decided to take the longer route, the one around the hovel's southside going north. He needed time for the wind to dry the tears on his cheeks. He took a few steps into the night's darkness, when he stumbled over Rover's body. "Rover, old boy? What is wrong with you?" Pete waited for a cloud to pass, and in the moonlight saw Rover had been shot. Where could he put Rover so Joey would not see. The southeast border had not been cleared. He carried Rover and placed him behind a hedge. Then went to bring the family home.

"There is Pete." Elisa shouted and walked towards him with Joey sleeping in her arms.

"Merci. We were in a frenzy of worry. Has anything happened to Andy?" Marie immediately asked. Pete was glad she could not see his face. Glad he could not see his mother's eyes in the darkness. "Nothing, mom. Shocked, yes. He found the house a total mess." Pete glanced at Joey, asleep in Elisa's arms. "I found Rover shot in the head." Pete rambled at words. "I will bury Rover tomorrow. Tell Joey. Suppose we should tell Joey. Tell him in the excitement, Rover ran off into the woods."

"Here I sit. Where have you all been?" Asked Andy.

Pete looked intently at him and ordered, "We will all go to bed. Face this mess in the morning."

From the open doorway the moon's filmy glow lightened the interior. Marie threw her arms outward and shrieked, "Look at this. I must clean. No one can sleep in this dirty upheaval and horrid smell. It is lager and . . ." Pete interrupted her, raised his arm and pointed to her sleeping room. "You and dad go into that room and go to sleep. We have had enough for today."

Marie stared at Pete. He never angrily yelled orders to her. She struggled between shock and tears, but walked in her balkiest manner to a chest, took a candle from the drawer, lit it and went to her room, not speaking a word. Her screams made Andy jump from his chair. "Sit, dad." Ordered Pete as he ran to his mom.

Marie leaned against Pete, shaking and sobbing. Rumpled bed coverings spotted with blood and mud were on the bed and floor. The matt had been slashed, exposing more bloodied straw. Pete soothenly, patted his mother and kissed her forehead. He flung the bloody covers into a heap. Yanked and pulled out the bloodied flax. He pushed any clean straw back into the matt and flipped it over. "There you are mom. Now get to bed."

Pete gathered the soiled material into his arms and left her standing alone, sobbing. Pete tossed the bloody mess into the fire. He turned to Andy, handed him his cane and helped him from the chair. "Mom is in there crying. Soldier's blood on the bedding upset her." Andy left, and squeezed Pete's hand, but said nothing.

"Lisa, you wait, while I check our bedding."

She stood, silently rocking Joey back and forth in her arms. Lisa spotted the broken, half-burned cradle in the fireplace and tears rolled down her cheeks. The cradle would hold no more babies. She had miscarried Artie. Would she cradle no more enfants. Was Joey to be her only child?

Pete rose before dawn to bury Rover. He finished at sunrise as rays sped upward, spreading light over the land. He opened both lower and upper doors and hoped the moist, fresh pre-dawn air would cleanse the stench before the others awoke. First, he removed the smelling pail beside the door and grabbed a spade leaning against the house and went a distance away. He dug furiously, until he had made a large pit, for scattered upon the hovel's floor was more excrement. As he dumped the pail's contents into the hole, Pete remembered the story Daniel once told about the king's chaise percee (commode). How the royal function of bringing the king his pot was considered an honorary duty, since these men had daily contact with the king. Each man seeking the mundane position had to prove an unbroken line of noble ancestry through seventeen generations of both father and mother. Pete shook his head and muttered, "That is real shit."

Heap by heap, shovelful by shovelful, Pete buried the trivial evidence of man's regressive human actions. He took tools from the stable and repaired Andy's broken rocker. Marie awakened and came into the room. "Merci. Look at Andy's books. I will have to get him."

"No. Let him rest. Crawling through the tunnel was a struggle for him."

"My word, yes. In this excitement, I never gave it a thought."

Pete put the rocker upright. "Has a bit of a jerk as it rocks, otherwise it seems fine." Marie was too busy looking around the room and picking up scattered pottery shards, scrapes of food, and chicken bones. "Wonder if I have any chickens left? Here is your Toby jug, broken into pieces."

Pete located the table's missing leg and worked at fixing the joint. Marie was carefully picking up pieces of Toby pottery, when Andy limped into the room. "Lucky I kept my cane with me. Looks as though they damaged everything in sight."

Marie sadly said, "Your books, dear. What a shame." Andy hobbled over to his rocker, commenting, "Thought I saw this broken."

"Pete fixed it."

"A-ha." He remarked and quickly sat; happy to reclaim ownership. Pete pointed to the mud around the hearth. "Appears from this mud, soldier's used your books to scrape mud from their boots." Back in his rocker, Andy had resigned himself to the situation. He glared at his books. "If their minds can not function, their feet must.

Our soldiers showed a bit of logic. Will not quibble over that." Andy took out his knife and began scraping mud from the books.

Entering the room, Daniel grumbled, "See no humor in vandalizing books. They all had knives and bayonets, or could have used the logs to scrape their boots."

Pete glanced at the fireplace and spotted the uncharred portion of the cradle and tugged at it. "All these logs stacked nearby and they have to burn this."

"Son, save that. Put it in the stable. I will rebuild it." Beneath the cradle were papers not totally burned. Pete took a closer look, "They burned all your Ramblers."

"You think French soldiers welcome a paper printed in England?" Pete was relieved to hear his dad's hearty laughter. Then he saw Elisa and Joey walk into the room. "Lisa, you and Joey sit in our one, and only, chair and eat breakfast while I repair the others."

Marie said, "Breakfast will be skimpy. Foodstuffs are gone. Troops found the rope-pull and emptied the step cellar. My urn of ground grain is gone and the bag I hung in the stable. I was hoping to make bread today."

"Mom, after I finish repairing these chairs, I will get the ladder and get into the ceiling-cellar. It should replenish our foodstuffs."

Elisa saw the goat in the stable, rose and sat Joey upon the chair. "Soldiers milked Bossie, but missed the goat. I am going to milk." Marie turned from washing dirty plates to face Andy and Pete. "Just think, if the soldiers knew these were English Sheffield plates, I would not have them to wash."

"Not if they knew they were English. Probably thought they were tin." Andy momentarily stopped scraping. "We have much to be thankful. House was not burned."

"Merci." Marie gasped and resumed her chore. Elisa returned carrying a gun in one hand and a pail of milk in the other. She handed the gun to Pete, "A soldier sleeping in the stable forgot his gun."

"Now, we have two guns. I already checked the stable. They did not find my gun." Andy shouted gleefully. Pete examined the gun, "Looks to be in fine shape."

"Let me have a look." Said Daniel.

"Have you a clean cup?" Marie handed Rita a tin cup, "Mighty happy to see that milk. I can make porridge." Elisa filled Joey's cup and noticed the table top. "Look at this. The table is covered with carved initials. Here are Joey's." Suddenly she remembered the silhouette. "Has anyone seen my silhouette? I kept it in this box, on this shelf, right here."

Andy fearfully sneaked a glance towards the fireplace ashes to see if it had been burned; then glanced upward to the mantel. The framed silhouette leaned against the wall. "Elisa, it is on the mantel."

She hastily went to the hearth, hoping to put it back into the box. Her reaching stopped in mid-air. She squealed, "Look. Come, look at this." Pete set his tools aside. Daniel laid the gun down. Andy laid a book away. Marie dried her hands. Everyone rushed to Elisa's side. "Wan-ta see. Me too." Begged Joey. Pete picked him up.

In messmerized silence, the family stared at the silhouette. The soldiers had emptied their pockets of coins, along with military medals and a rabbit's foot, and placed them around the framed silhouette. No one spoke but Joey, who popped his finger from his mouth and gleefully pointed to the silhouette.

"Dat me, mommie. Dat's me."

CHAPTER 8: WAR IS OVER

Monty awakened, surprised he had managed to sleep. In the blackness of the pit he could not tell if it was morning. Except for snorings and the sea's constant beat against the hull, the pit was silent. The odor was gaseous, and he was afraid to cough for fear of opening his mouth to unhealthy and diseased air. A baby cried and its mother quickly nursed it, for it became quiet. The cry awakened most of the passengers, and there was jostling as people tried to stretch themselves from cramped positions. Finally, the steerage door opened. The rising sun blinded the passengers as they left the pit for breakfast.

Monty inhaled the refreshing salty air. His eyes took awhile to adjust to the welcomed light, and before him lay the shimmering, glistening ocean, the horizon and the sky. His view was interrupted by stomach spasms of vomiting. Monty watched the ship's wake cut the ocean's glassy surface, as he walked the deck through the crowded maze of people. He saw a woman collapse after vomiting, and lodge herself precariously near the deck's edge. One rocking movement of the ship would cast her overboard. He rushed to her side, grabbed her and hung to the post-rail.

"Let me die. I am so sick." The girl pleaded.

"Silly talk. You will feel better. Lean on my shoulder. Breathe this nice sea air." She turned towards his shoulder and Monty recognized her. "I remember you. You were in the coach to St. Brieuc."

"Never should have gone. Never should have. . . Oh, I am so sick."

"It will wear off." He reached in his vest pocket and removed some paraffin. "Chew this. My mother added a peppermint herb to it. It will help. What is your name?"

"Teresa Bordeau. What is yours?"

"Simon Regnier. Call me Monty."

"I can not go back into that atrocious pit."

"We can stay on deck, but we will have to return at dusk."

"I can not. Just can't."

"We will go together. You will not be alone."

"I left my aunt and got on this ship, thinking America would be so marvelous."

"It is. We will be there, eventually."

"Do you really think so? Will this come to an end?"

"Yes. Then all will be worthwhile."

"How long do you suppose this sickness will last?"

"I think you have another day. Tell me about yourself."

"What a mistake. Thought I would leave home because there are so many mouths to feed. My father has not found work in this Industrial Revolution. Leave home. Work as a housekeeper in America and return home with money."

"Where is home?"

"Paris."

"My home is in Le Mans. When we land in New York, I plan to take the railroad to Chicago. What is your destination?"

"I do not know. Probably stay in New York."

Monty noticed her flaxen hair, and how the damp air had made ringlets around her forehead. The glow in her cheeks had returned and her lips were a pouty, cupid's bow. He remembered her bright blue eyes. She was frail and dependant. Monty felt a desire to protect her.

"Best, we move to the opposite railing where we do not face the sun. It can burn you badly."

Teresa felt safer by his side and followed Monty. They talked until the sun moved over the ship and cast its shadow on the opposite side.

"It must be noon. Do you feel like eating?"

"Yes. I am saving this paraffin." She took it from her mouth and put it into her bodice. "Do you suppose bread and water is all we are going to get on this voyage? How I would like soup."

"I think so. We are being treated like prisoners. Drinking from cups passed from passenger to passenger, really worries me. No telling what diseases are being spread."

"How are we going to stand this day-after-day?"

"Maybe by stories. Here is the captain now with lunch. Let us go." Teresa and Monty, drank their water and went to the rail to eat their rolls. They were gazing at the shinning water, when Teresa asked, "What did you mean when, stories may help us cope?"

"Stories about my ancestors. Stories told to me by my grandpere and pere, seem to help me; and has made time pass more quickly."

"I know nothing about my ancesters, other than my grandparents.

They did not tell stories of the past."

"Really? How odd. My life has been filled with stories from one generation to the next."

"Tell me one of your stories. I can think about it during the awful night ahead."

For his ancestors to come alive, Monty, only had to recall. He gazed at the rambling white clouds in the horizon.

"Monty, tell me a story? You say your name is Simon. Let me hear a Simon says. Simon says. Simon says . . ." Whined Teresa.

"I am thinking. There is no way I can express myself, but to pretend my ancestors are living. I self-motivate myself to discover them from stories told to me. Then with a little dialogue, they take shape."

"I understand. Tell me. Want to hear. Simon says . . ."

"I shall begin with Lambert Andre's family. He was called Andy. Peter, his son, had planned to hunt."

"Now, Monty, begin as I asked, with Simon says." He smiled at Teresa and began the story again.

"Simon says . . .

"Wanna go. Wanna hunt with daddy." Joey pleaded. Pete put the gun down, bent over to look into his face, "Joe old boy, it is too cold. But soon, it will be warmer. Then we will go." Joey hung his head. He did not like being rebuffed. It was one of those times he preferred being called Joey, instead of Joe. He sensed the different treatment which came with each name--leniency with Joey and discipline with Joe.

"You are not going to wave goodbye to daddy?" Joey gave a lingering wave. "Joe, shut that door. You are letting the cold inside." Elisa added.

"Joey, come over here. You and I will have a reading session." Said Daniel.

"Sum-won com-un. Sum-wom com-un." Shouted Joey, still peeking at his dad from the door. Elisa dashed to the door, "Why it is Louise, Jacque's wife. Merci. Hope nothing has happened to Jacque."

"Louise, come in and warm yourself." Marie guided her to a chair. Louise joyously flung her cap and shed her mittens onto the table. "The war is over. Just heard. The treaty has been signed."

"Can it be true?" Asked Marie. Elisa picked up Joey and danced around singing, "Glory, glory." Andy sighed, "Amen."

"How is Jacque?" Asked Andy.

"Oh, he is all right. I made him stay home as I can walk faster."

"Louise, did you tell, Pete?"

"Yes. Met him by the garden plot. I must get back. Jacque and I are celebrating with wine. Brought you a bottle."

"Godspeed and tell Jacque, merci." Said Marie. "Tell Jacque we will pop the cork when Pete returns." Glibbed Andy, happily.

"Me too? Have wine. I be three." Joey held up his chubby three fingers.

The women grabbed each other's hands, then Daniel's and Joey's as they circled, pranced round and round singing until they plopped into chairs exhausted. Andy's bad leg kept him from joining.

"You women best stir up some fixings for a celebration dinner." Said Daniel.

"Yes." Both women answered in unison. Joyously they giggled, chattered, and clinked cooking utensils. "If Pete does not come home with a rabbit, we will splurge with a ham from the rafter cellar." Murmured Marie giddily.

Elisa handed Joey a basket. "Would you get some apples from the step-cellar for me?"

"Mommie, I do the job."

Upon hearing the news, Daniel's elation overpowered his being. He felt weightless in his comfortable rocker. He felt healed of all physical aches and his rocking motion soon put him to sleep.

Joey gave the basket to Elisa and tugged on Marie's apron. "Gampa's sleeping. He not read to me."

"Shhh, be quiet now, Joey. The exciting good news and our ring-around-the-rosy tired him." Marie tip-toed over to the rocker and lifted a book from Daniel's lap.

Elisa stooped to better talk to Joey, "Thank you son for the apples. You think the puppies are lonesome?" Joey frowned. "I go luv-um."

"You keep them in the stable. Do not let them into the room."

"No. Make gampa mad."

"It will make us all mad."

After Andy had poured wine, he said, "Now, we give toasts. Joey, come here and join us in the toast. Is there milk in your cup?"

"Got milk. Want wine." Answered Joey, curling his bottom lip into a pout.

"Here is your wine, dad."

"Best, you let him sleep,"

"Then, we are ready to toast this glorious, blessing?" Said Andy.

"War gone." Said Joey.

"Let us raise our drinks in a toast to the end of wars."

"You shout at ta dinner table, grandpere."

It was a joyous toast, but saddened for Daniel did not awaken.

A year had passed since Daniel's death. Death bewildered little Joey. What Joey understood was his great grandpere, his hand-squeezing-buddy was gone. He thought Daniel would be with him forever. Joey accepted, but did not like what grandpere Andy told him. "Daniel missed great grandmere Diane, and left to join her in paraiso--heavon."

"You will not leave me, will you grandpere?" Andy restrained smarting tears and struggle to feign composure. "Joey, do not worry about tomorrows. Enjoy your todays. Do you understand?"

"Wake up and be happy until bedtime?" Joey asked.

"That is right, Joey. You are a smart little thinker. I am proud of you."

"Tell me about America, grandpere. Tell Indian story."

"Another one? Don't you tire of them?"

"No, why Indians not live in our woods?"

"Because their mothers and fathers live in America."

"Tell story, grandpere."

"Well, over across the sea, in far off America, lives an Ottawa Indian."

"His name, grandpere. What is his name?"

"Chief Pontiac, he liked to listen to his old, wise friend, Neolin; who kept saying their people should not change their old ways or land. He told Chief Pontiac to fight."

"Who he fight?"

"White people." Answered Andy, sorry he had gotten into the subject and anticipating Joey's next question, added, "Because they were coming into their land and wanting them to use our ways."

"What Chef Pon-tack do, grandpere?"

"He decided to fight and attacked the British Ft. Detroit. Then other Indian tribes. . . ."

"Tybes? What are Tybes, grandpere?"

"Indian tribes are different groups of different families."

"Like Fr. Mo-rows church?"

"Well, yes, in a way. Now after Pontiac. . . ."

"Chef Pon-tack, grandpere."

"Yes, after Chief Pontiac's attack at Detroit. . . ."

"Fut Troit, grandpere."

"That is right, Fort Detroit. The other Indian tribes decided to join Chief Pontiac in fighting the white people, who kept coming and coming."

"Who deez peeple, grandpere?"

"People who leave here and cross the sea to build new homes."

"Who are deez tybes that fight? How many, grandpere?"

"Oh my, let me see. There are seven. The Shawnee, Chippewa, Huron, Lenni Lanape, Miami, and the Potawattomie."

"Grandpere, dat's six, not seven."

"And the Senecas." Said Andy, as he scratched his beard in exasperation.

"Doz are funny woids, grandpere."

"You suppose they think our words sound funny? Some tribes learned French, English and Spanish."

"Oui, I think 'mouche' (fly) is a funny word. More story, grandpere."

"There were alot of battles until England proclaimed the white people could not go past the tops of the Appalachian Mountains."

"Mountuns higher dan da Alps?"

"Joey, I do not know. I think not. Anyway, England thought the law would stop the fighting."

"Did it, grandpere?"

"No, but France gave all the land west of the Mississippi River to Spain."

"Wiff-er, have funny name, too. Why our King give land away?"

"Because Spain was on our side, and helped us fight in the war. Now, off to bed."

Peter saw Andy struggling to walk and jumped up to help. "Do not need help. I am only exaggerating, to show how it feels to have Joey pull and drain a story from you."

"I have often thought Joey should have been named after the Attester."

The men lit pipes and settled in their rockers. "You know, it amazes me Joey's interest is the same as the reading Parisian fad for the American frontier, Indians, and people called cowboys. It is the most popular topic in Paris." Said Pete.

"Shows their reading level--that of a child." Said Elisa.

"Several times, I told Trina, Job's wife, who works at their bookstore, I would like books on the American frontier in order to keep up with Joey's story demands. She told me every time Job goes to Paris for books, the frontier books have been sold. They cannot keep up with the demand." Said Andy.

Pete pointed to an article in the paper. "I would think, there would be more interest in the political discussions raging over in England about America, than in tales about the American frontier. On page two, it says Josiah Tucker, an English political economist, claims driving France out of America would be a fatal mistake as the colonists would then seek independence. He is being ridiculed for his claim."

Andy bent his head back in thought, "That is a good question. I have never thought about it. They are definitely loyal subjects, but could change."

Pete laid the paper in his lap, "I read in this Rambler, Britain's generosity to its defeated rival was due to replacing William Pitt with Lord Bute."

"What difference did that make?" Asked Pete.

"Seems, answered Andy, "Lord Bute wanted a balance of European powers. His theory angered William Pitts and a radical named, John Wilkes, but the English people are to war-weary to take much notice. It is costly shouldering their armed presence in America, and there is little paid in trade duties. This is the interesting part. English customs service paid out four times more in salaries to their collectors than what was taken in from duties. Claims it was the reason why British Parliament passed the Revenue Act, called the Sugar Act, and then passed a Currency Act."

This news surprised Andy, "Maybe Josiah Tucker will prove to be right. If England starts taxing to cover their costs of being over there, it could cause revolt."

The war had forced France to acknowledge British supremacy in North America and India. King Louis XVI and Queen Marie Antoinette continued to ignore France's political and economic effects and statecraft, and lived lavishly. More than in the past, the years brought hardships and dangers. Famine, taille, and disease continued and rebellious thoughts infected all of France.

People tired of hearing and reading about Paris, with its people of ton with their wit and gaiety, coupled with precieuses, to hide their obscene manners. Novelty was the rage among the aristocracy, and current events were of no concern.

Without the bond and companionship of Daniel, the past two years had been difficult for Joey. Joey was full of questions. Questions, great grandpere Daniel always had the time, and been around to answer. Grandpere Andy told him stories but now, at six, he had lessons with Father Moreau. Hard lessons. Not the fun of great-grandpere's lessons.

Joe systematically picked berries from his porridge and piled them to the side. "Joe, eat those berries." Said Elisa.

"Why do I have to eat them? Great grandpere would not make me eat those."

"You are too full of questions."

"Awh Mom, they are seedy. Do not want them."

"Remember, stories grandpere told about Captain John Cook who discovered Hawaii?"

"Yes. He sailed the seas. Got into a fight and was killed by Hawaiians."

"I read where Captain Cook's seamen were dying from a disease called scurvy, and . . ."

"Scurvy? What is that?"

"Captain Cook discovered it was caused from his sailors not having fresh berries and garden food. The disease rots your teeth and makes festering sores on your skin."

"I do not want sores." Said Joe as he began eating his discarded berries.

"Son, you are running late, today is your lesson. I will feed the chickens this morning." Said Pete.

"Phooey, I get tired of those books and things. I want to do farmwork."

"Joey, it is all you will be able to do, if you do not learn to read and write. You are not being taught to be a puppet as the boys in noble families, drilled by dancing masters and taught fake airs and manners of snobbery. Now, more than ever, is a time in Europe when you must learn to read, for any book written in French is read by people over the entire continent. Now hurry along." Said Pete.

"Can I take the dogs?"

"Yes, but tie them up when you get there."

"Mom, can I take this basket? Coming home from my last lesson, I saw a patch of blackberries along the path. I will pick some for you."

Joey was learning to read at the time when France's power and prestige influenced the continent, as did the spread and usage of the French culture and language. Reading and a common language also made possible propaganda, discussion and critical comment. Writing stimulated enlightenment ideas. The idea every man should be free and happy, crept into minds of thinkers and began to make changes in administration, educational and economic matters. Conflicts and impact from enlightened thinkers often affected the Church, especially from inside Habsburg dominions and Voltaire's attacks. Philosophers attacked religion with its scandals such as the Calas' execution at Toulouse. It was Jean Jacques Rousseau, who stirred souls and renewed religious faith.

The family was waiting to eat their noon meal when Joe returned with a basket of shiny blackberries. "Here, Mom. Father Moreau said we make a living by what we get, but we make a life by what we give."

"Joe, wise words, all right. You gave your mother nice berries and she gave you news about scurvy. But, if she could not read, she would not have the knowledge to share, now would she? How were your other lessons?" Asked Pete.

"The best part was when he showed me the painting done by the man who did those pictures in my books of Don Quioxte and The Vicar of Wakefield."

"Daniel Chodowiecki. You study, and someday you will be able to read those books. Not just admire the engravings."

"What was the painting called?" Asked Elisa.

"The Parting of Jean Calas from his Family."

"It is a sad bit of history."

"I know. It was the lesson today. Had to write a story about it."

"That is good." Said Pete. "Nawh, it is not. I do not like writing. It bothers me when I write. This thing on my finger."

"What? Let me see your hand. Why, Pete, look at his finger."

"Is it scurvy?" Moaned Joey.

"No, son. It is a wort. A growth."

"Do not like it, dad. Can you cut it off?"

"We will try my grandmere's remedy." Said Elisa.

"Lisa, not one of those old lunar folk myths and superstitions." Sighed Pete.

"Pete, if you cut the wort off during time of a full moon, it will be hard to stop the bleeding. Joey, we will watch for the first full moon, and then you go outside in the moon's rays and blow on the wort nine times."

"Lisa. Do not fill the boy's mind with nonsense. It will not work. But, Joey do as your mom asks, and then I will cut it off."

"Pete, if you cut it off, be sure you do it on the moon's day, a Monday."

CHAPTER 9: HODGEPODGE

"Enough story-telling. There is the captain. Let us go get our rolls."

"What a funny story. I have not laughed for such a long time. Laugh and vomit, what a combination. Will you tell me another one this afternoon." Said Teresa.

"Yes. Grab your roll and come to the deck-rail, where we can talk and vomit."

"You have the nicest laugh."

Monty thought, she likes my smile. I will please her with another story. You munch on your roll, while I tell you a story. As you say, Teresa,

Simon says . . . "

"Elisa, tomorrow Mike needs to go into Paris, and he does not want to go alone. We will probably stop awhile at the village tavern. Do you need anything?"

"Paris? It is dangerous, Pete. The king is so hated, there is fear of a revolution, and he built that wide-circled road around Paris in order to avoid the city. Everyone is talking about violence between Catholics and Protestants, to say nothing about the rebellious half-clothed, starving street people."

"Lisa, the violence is in southern France. As for the street people, we will be in the northwest end of the eighteenth arrondissment, where the junk dealers and rag pickers are. Mike thinks he can find tool parts he needs among the junk dealers Besides, the Duc de Choiseul is running France, not the king."

"You be home before sunset?"

"Yes, do not worry."

While Joe, a boy of seven, was being taught by Jesuits, so was another young boy. Marquis de Marie Joseph Gilbert Motier Lafayette lived for eleven years with his grandmother and aunt, and was being taught by a village priest in southern France. A ten year old, lord of the manor in the secluded forests of Chavaniac at the Chateau de Chavaniac. Wild animals populated the area, and wolves prowled in hungry packs up to peasants' lowly hovels. It was an inhospitable region where few huntsmen chose to enter. Here, Pete and Mike returned from Paris and stopped at Ye Olde Yoke. "Mike, our tavern gang is sitting over at the far table."

"Mike, we were wondering if you would be in today." Said Mike Slagger.

"We just came from Paris. I picked up tool parts and junk I think can be turned into a plow."

"Pete, what is going on in the City of Light?" Asked Phillip Tudoreau.

"I can tell you this much, to see Paris is an experience I will not forget. Feelings you can not get from reading the papers. Police raids going on from sunrise to sunset. The aristocracy claim the raids are due to hunger-driven, lazy, riffraff from all over France into Paris. But we learned from a merchant, the truth. The more raids, the more pay-offs to police. He said the high living cost was producing graft in the lower levels of city administration."

"No grain to be seen in the markets, anywhere." Added Mike Gautier.

"We know Pompadour's physician, Dr. Quesnay, is responsible for preventing private grain sales until the state meets the army's needs, and for the high grain prices at ports." Said Mike Slagger.

"What? Why is he doing that?" Asked Pete, as he recalled his early admiration of Quesnay.

Phillip answered, "For monies to fill the king's pockets at our expense."

"I have not had grain to mill for sometime. Do not know what we would have done without the farm." Said Karl Brener.

"Read this." Mike Gautier handed a paper to Jacque Richelieu. "We were on the street and handed this pamphlet telling of the king's plan to starve his people. And we had not walked far, when an emaciated man, his face distorted by hate, handed us another pamphlet. It was so vile, I tossed it away."

"What was it about?" Asked John Dumier.

"About the goings on at the Parc-aux-Cerfs. Remember when old lady Pompadour had it built with little pavilions in the park and the high wall around it? In her old age, she did not want any rival, so in order to please the king, she had her agents collect ten to twelve year old girls from every port in France for the king. She has been dead four years, but it is still going on. The hawkers on the streets shouted lampoons as they passed out this paper, and yelled the trade was between six to seven thousand little girls. Absolutely, sickening. I ask you, is that a king for France?" Roared Mike Gautier.

"Hell, he should be castrated." Said Otto Schmiller.

As Pete turned off the Paris road, onto the road to his hovel, he hollered, "Mike, I will leave you here. Hope you get home before sunset."

"Pete, I was beginning to get worried."

"Lisa, Mike got his material and we are home safe and sound without any danger. Same old stuff. More hawkers shouting discontent. As we walked past the antique shops, I saw the most beautiful clock. It was far too expensive. Otherwise, I would have bought it."

"Oh, I want to hear. Tell me about it."

"It was sculptured in bronze on an onyx base. The clock-part sat between two oval, mahogany bases topped with this beautiful statue of an Indian warrior on a log raft with his wounded wife. He was rowing her to safety. She held an arrow in her right hand. Made me think of the Treaties of Fort Stanwix between the Iroquois Indians where England gave them gifts worth $10,000 for the immense chunk of America. Bigger than France, it was. France is only 213,673 square miles."

It was the turn of another year, 1768, when the Marquis Lafayette, at eleven, went to live at his grandfather's hotel in Paris and enrolled at the College du Plessis. Joey at eight, was steadily progressing in his lessons.

"Pete, I learned something fascinating today." Said Elisa.

Pete laid his paper aside, "Andy, what do you suppose that can be?"

"Pete, you know I have always been partial to reading Carlo Goldoni's plays. In one of your Ramblers, I read where Goldoni is now tutoring the daughter of Louis XV. It made me feel smart to think royalty and I, a poor peasant, prefer the same choice in literature. Made me feel so good, I fixed your favorite tonight, kraut and neckbones."

Joey replied, "Momma, you know art, and you have always liked the painting, The Swing. At my last lesson, the priest spoke about how Jean Fragonard, now that he is older, no longer paints to suit the minds of the aristocracy's whims. He now paints realities. The governor has even provided him with a studio."

"That is interesting, son, but what was your lesson on?"

"The priest tole me, "People may doubt what you say, but they will believe what you do.' And I had to write about the meaning."

"You are not bothered with writing, now that the wort is gone?"

"No, I like it. It is as though I am talking to myself."

Andy stopped rocking to say, "I am so tired of this confining weather and this rocker; even the words I read, seem to hop up and down with my rocking."

"Maybe you better lay off the cider."

"My point is, I have come up with an interesting plan to break boredom."

"How is that, dad?"

"Use our wood and carving skills for gain. Read there is a great demand in America for hand-carved games of battledores, shuttlecocks, cricket balls, pellets, tennis racquets and backgammon tables. Josua Corrine's cousin, who supplies fish for his market, could take our carvings on his trips to the Le Havre merchants for export."

Pete said, "Making a backgammon table would be fun."

"Next trip into the village, I will ask Josua if we could make arrangements. In fact, I am going to start working on a chess set."

Josua agreed, for a nominal fee, to transport their woodworks. Andy's profits, he hide in a dried, leather pouch. He refused to tell his reason, but said he would reveal its purpose on his deathbed.

The continuing famine and tailles were physically taxing upon the French people. Paris was hit by the rising cost of living and in order to squeeze money from the arrested and innocent victims' families, the city was now having both night and daytime raids. Poverty drove many into Paris and one mob overpowered guards, stormed and ransacked the "palais" of the chief magistrate. France in 1770, was, itself, nationally deteriorating and the monarchy further rotting. Greed and money was king. All sorts of things were happening that money had purchased. Anything in France could be had for money.

Duc de Choiseul had arranged the marriage of Marie Antoinette to the Bourbons. In an effort to not share his power, he chose his sister, Duchesse de Grammont, as Pompadour's successor. In retaliation, his clerical rivals found Mme du Barry and due to her influence, she undermined Duc de Etienne Choiseul's position in court. Pompadour had been vengeful, Du Barry was not. But, Du Barry took money and gifts from people who wanted her to request things from the king. It was common for people wanting to do away with someone to pay for such a service. Du Barry kept "Lettres de cachet," signed by the king and money orders (acquits complaints) in her desk for easy disposal. Many innocent people were accused and killed through this blatant method of doing away with a person. Death was common among the poor, as well as high society, where uncleanliness was prevalent enough to cut lives short. Instead of washing and bathing, aristocrats used oils and ointments from the East. Rat bites were common and rats would travel, hidden in the dressfolds amongst the aristocrats' massive, layers of folded clothing. By 1771 Louis XIV had lost all his legitimate children, sons-in-law, grandsons and great-grandsons except one, from death.

Books were written on economics, starvation, and the bread crisis, and were topics of conversation even among the aristocrats, replacing the popular frontier stories of America. Commerce des bles, by Jacques Necker, a simple merchant, who had universal acclaim, was being quoted in awe and deep reverence. Necker's book on the grain trade aroused envy and was hotly attacked. Necker called for sacrifices and renunciation from the rich. Necker had no nobility, the status so required during these times, yet he had succeeded through his own talent and ability.

Joey, at ten, was reading the Rambler and understanding too much of the world's evils. His ideals of America took a tumble when he read about the Boston Massacre. America was a world of his dreamland and a place to habor fanciful dreams.

Layfayette, of noble birth, during his childhood had witnessed the peasant's lowly lot in Auvergne and had resolved to take the side of the poor. Necker intrigued Lafayette and intrigued Joe. The two young strangers, Joey and Lafayette, grew up listening to talk and studying about the famous man, Necker.

"Joe, you are late." Said Rita.

"Father Moreau assigned a report and I stayed at the library to write it."

"What did you write about?" Asked Pete.

"Our navigator, Louis Antoine de Bougainville."

"Did you know that he also served in the Seven Years War?"

"No. I wrote about his adventures going around the world."

"Oh, then you have read his book, A Voyage Round the World?"

"Yes, it was one of the new books in the parish library."

In 1772, the new frontier in France was Metz; headed by Duc de Broglie and occupied by a heavily armed garrison.

"This morning I am going to the village. I heard news about Poland being annexed by Russia, Prussia and Austria. I want to pay David Portier's family a visit. Rebecca must be worried sick about her family in Poland. Will take along some of my cheeses." Said Elisa.

"I better go with you. They live a distance from the village. Dad, you and Joe can handle the chores."

"Yes, Joe can handle the livestock while I hoe the field." Said Andy.

Elisa knocked on the Portier's door. "Greetings, we came to bring you some cheese and express our concerns. Have you any further news from Poland?" Rebecca motioned them to sit, "David is in the field. I will call him."

"Do not bother him. Our visit will be short."

"News? No, not a word. I hope my family is in the Austrian partition of the annexation. I have no knowledge on how the bounderies were divided, have you, Pete?"

"No, I do not, Rebecca. If I hear I will get word to you."

"There are frightening stories everywhere. Germany is no place to be, either." Rebecca lamented. Pete nodded in agreement, "I have heard stories the king's brother, Duke of Gloucester, has been spreading about England's King George III. It is rumored the king is going mad."

"Surely not." Replied Elisa.

Rebecca spoke up, "He is right. I heard it from Catherine when in her milliner's shop. She whispered so her customers would not hear."

"All along, Andy has said the man's insane." Said Pete.

"How would he know?" Asked Elisa.

"I think dad's judgment is correct for two reasons. Tthe king could have disposed of the Boston uprising without firing a musket, but did not. He could have granted, instead of refusing, the right of English citizens to not pay taxes, except taxes granted by their elected representatives and thus, satisifed the emigrants. But no, he killed them. He instigated a trading of recruits with German princes to sell subjects at so much a head. Is that the actions of a sane man?"

"We have got to leave. Give our regards to David."

Elisa and Pete had no sooner entered their hovel, when Joey burst through the door, sobbing and sped into his sleeping room.

"My word, what do you suppose has happened, Pete?" Asked Elisa.

"I will sure find out." Said Pete, and left to talk with Joey. The longer Elisa waited, the more disturbed she became, and hustled to brew a pot of tea. She was waiting for the tea, when Pete entered with tears in his eyes. "Joey did not have his lesson today because Father Moreau died. I am going to the field to tell dad."

Father Moreau's funeral had been a month ago. Andy and Pete

were in the stable when Andy noticed Pete was feeding, yet paying no attention to ol' Ox. Usually, he scratched and spoke to ol' Ox.

"Why so glum?"

"Since Joey turned thirteen, I am getting more concerned about European conditions than our harvest needs."

"That is every father's lament, son."

"But dad, France is on the verge of civil war and in Russia, the Cossacks are rebelling against Catherine the Great."

"You talking about the Cossack leader, Yemelyan Pugachov?"

"That is right."

Andy chuckled and said, "You know he claims to be the assassinated Tsar Peter III?" Pete laughed as he scratched the ears of ol' Ox.

Later that evening, Andy puffed on his pipe and threw a paper to Pete in his rocker. "The Rambler says Yemelyan Pugachov was beheaded."

"That is the end of Tsar Peter III."

"That is horrid, why are you men laughing? You do not make sense. Tsar Peter III was assassinated?" Asked Elisa.

"You are right Lisa, he was assassinated. It is a private joke."

"Well, you men get yourselves to the table, Joey's already reaching for the cheese."

Pete put down the paper and no sooner had seated himself, than he began. "Here it is 1774, and still our French reign's squabbling continues. I put alot of hope in the efforts of Turgot and Necker, trying to implement reforms, but opposition from Marie Antoinette and the aristocracy allowed them no headway. What is it going to take, to wake up our Court from its decaying sleep? Rebellion? The Russian revolt is over, will France be next?"

"Now, eat your supper and calm down, or you will surely get an attack of gout." Elisa whined.

"Threat of civil war is enough to give anyone the gout. Must confess, I have even thought of immigrating."

"Do you mean that, dad?" At fourteen, Joey found any hint of adventure enticing and America fascinating. Andy thought of his leather pouch and smiled.

"He does not." Elisa scowled at Pete.

"No, son. I am almost thirty-three. Feel half my lifetime has been spent. Immigrating is an opportunity for the young."

Andy reached for the crackers. "Joey, there is a time and place for immigration. Now, for instance, the people of Wales have the time, place and opportunity. King James of England had his secretary, Robert Cecil, invite people of Wales to move to England. He promised free land, no taxes, exemption from military service for two-hundred years, and allowed them to keep their traditions and language."

"That would be hard to refuse, considering they have had over population and famine." Added Pete.

"I managed to find news, not so grim." Said Elisa.

"Good news, would be news."

"Mom, what was the good news?"

"Louis XVI is discussing the idea of making the Louve into a museum."

Pete retorted, "Museum? Art for the starving instead of food?" Elisa frowned at him, and added, "A shadow theater is opening at Versailles. A type of shadow puppet drama, where black silhouettes are cast from puppets. It is called 'ombres chinoises' (Chinese shadows) because the art was brought here from the far East by European travelers."

Andy asked, "Who in their right mind would travel without a carriage into the streets of Paris to view works of art?"

"Oh, you old grouches. You are glad our beloved painter, Jacques David, won the Prix de Rome, aren't you?"

"That is good news."

"I have some good news. An English painter, George Morland, a boy of only ten, has already exhibited sketches at the Royal Academy. A boy of ten, can you imagine?" Marie asked.

"No." Andy replied.

"What do you mean, no?"

"I mean no, woman. How can I imagine, or be impressed when I have not seen the boy's sketches?"

Joe was fifteen when his grandmere Marie died. The year when Benjamin Franklin fled from London to Paris at the outbreak of the American Revolution. The French called Franklin, "Lightning tamer," and adored him. Jewelers put his portrait on snuffboxes and fobs. In America, John Paul Jones, commander of the navy was capturing and sinking many ships. News reached France, George Washington suffered a devastating defeat. Monsieur de Beaumarchais was delivering worn out shooting irons and rusty sabers to American buyers for his own profit.

Elisa spread the Rambler upon the table and read, "See here, where it publicly states that King George III is permanently insane."

Pete replied, "Let's talk about a man, worthy of being a king--

young Lafayette."

"I have heard only good words about him. I know he, too, admires Necker." Said Joe.

"Believe those words."

"Pete, I just question his closeness to that gad-about, Comte d' Artois. Everyone knows the king pays the debts for his extravagant brothers, Comte d'Artois and Charles X Provence, but does not trust either one. Monsieur Provence is sickly, intelligent, well-read, and a passionate monarchist. Comte d' Artois is not as intelligent, but athletic, a gambler, clothes-horse and woman-chaser."

"Andy, of course, he would have a childhood bond with Comte d'Artois. They had riding lessons together during their youth."

"Where did you hear that?" Elisa asked.

"From Mike Gautier, who takes his horse to our blacksmith, Bonet. Bonet heard it from the blacksmith, Charles Antoine, who runs a Paris livery."

"My word, and you men say you do not gossip."

"I thought we were discussing Lafayette." Muttered Pete, and continued. "Marquis Lafayette is the son of a fallen comrade of De Broglie's army at Hastenbeck. Jacque told me. You know that was where Jacque lost his leg. Jacque said for a young sprout, Lafayette was highly admired for his character and fearless leadership, and was a cavalry captain at age seventeen."

Andy chuckled, saying, "As Lisa, would say, I heard some gossip when in the bookstore. Job told me Lafayette, the liberty-minded, had no desire for the Court. Lafayette's father-in-law secured for his son-in-law, the opportunity for an appointment to serve as Monsieur Provence's chamberlain. Lafayette could not afford to offend his wife's father; so he figured out a clever, tactical means to offend and dissuade Monsieur Provence from naming him to the post."

"How did he do that?" Joe asked.

"It is comical, but clever. At the next Court ball he put his wig on crookedly and sloppily so a batch of his red hair blatantly showed. He followed Monsieur Provence around the ballroom, mocking him in spiteful fashion. Monsieur Provence became angry and shouted he would remember his remarks. Lafayette acting as though he was not recognizable, said his final insult by quoting Shakespeare."

"What did he say?" Elisa eagerly asked.

"Memory is the wit of fools." Answered Andy and added, "Needless to say, he was not appointed and had not offended his father-in-law by refusing the unwanted post."

"I will tell you something, but it must not be repeated." Said Pete. "You know Josua Corrine has contacts with the ports through his fish-market business, and he told me this in strictest confidence. Josh said fishermen were talking about when Lafayette heard of Ben Franklin's troubles, he offered to buy an ocean-going vessel for one-hundred francs in order to transport supplies and recruited officers to Boston. Old Ben did not want Lafayette to engage in such a danger, and explained their meeting and plan had gone undetected, only because Lord Stormont recently considered the English rebellion over. He disbanded some of his espionage operations, including the one previously required of listing visitors received by Franklin. He warned and reminded Lafayette, France wanted to stay on amiable terms with England; and thus England had increased their guard of the French government and Lord Stormont still had spies in every seaport."

"Is that all the story? What happened?" Asked Elisa.

"The point was to show you how much Ben Franklin thinks of Lafayette. He said Lafayette's trip was postponed because he and his wife had volunteered to get vaccinated with the newly discovered inoculation against smallpox.

"Speaking of heros, how about Louis Bougainville? I remember as a kid, I wrote a paper on him. Now he's hailed as our most successful commander in the American Revolution."

"You are fifteen. No longer a kid?" Elisa asked. Joe gave his mother a sheepish grin. "At twelve I read his book, A Voyage Round The World."

CHAPTER 10: SO BE IT.

Monty vomited again, and Teresa gently held his head as he bent over the railing. Her tenderness stirred Monty's feelings, "Well, that put an end to the story. Do you want another?"

"Do you feel up to it?" Asked Teresa. Monty grinned and began.

"Simon says . . ."

Peter walked in the woods to strengthen his spirits. He came from the cemetery, down the path to stop and sit under the hickory tree. Joe was sixteen, a fact that pushed Peter into a type of time-jump. It was only yesterday, Joe was born; when Daniel and Diane were alive? He vaguely his grandparents, Peter and Maggie. The old had became lost in the ancient cycle of life. He sat, while recollections flashed through his mind of a time of yesterdays before children age and babes were borne.

France too, was aging, shifting from years of monarchistic and militant wars into a combustible social war of survival and ideation. In America, the final decisive action of the American Revolution had come when Generals Washington and Rochambeau moved troops south to Virginia where British Cornwallis had entrenced his troops in Yorktown at the mouth of the York River.

"One more should do it." Pete said, as he lifted the heavy maul and banged it down on a blade set carefully on the anvil.

"I have not yet loosened this blade." Joe tilted the long handle to a better position. "You are spending a lot of effort sharpening these scythes, considering there is little grain to harvest."

Pete dropped the maul upright upon the ground; sighed and looked at the woods. "Did not think I would see a time when our plan was not profitable enough to feed us. I keep thinking harvests can not get poorer, but each year has been worse than the last. Joe, remem ber, when the woods covered our losses?"

"Yes, I remember. Mom enjoyed the wooded reaping. You would tease her about roaming through flowers instead of working. It was before the wagons took more than their share and the animals had found our spots."

"Son, wildlife knew where our plantings were. Before, they

found enough to eat without bothering our crops. It was not until the famines began. Poor critters are starving, too, or roving hunters take them. Sad, very sad. Rabbits and deer have almost disappeared. The woods remind me of France, her people starving, being arrested and executed while ideals and glory wither and disappear. We will never know how many of our future geniuses and leaders have been killed, or ones never born. There is Lisa, clanging the dinner bell. Best, we make haste."

Joe slapped Pete on the shoulder. "You sound like grandpere."

"How is that?" Pete asked, and broke out in a pleased smile. "He always said, best this or best that."

"Guess, he did, son." The men walked towards the house. "You know how fussy mom is, best you brush the dirt off your breeches."

Elisa had the black kettle on the table, as it had been yesterday and would be tomorrow. Soup was a fortunate meal during the famine. Milk and bread were scarce luxuries few peasants enjoyed. Sitting down at the table, Elisa excitedly patted Pete's hand, "Guess what? The village is having a fair tomorrow. A traveling troupe from Paris. Margarite . . . "

Pete asked, "Who?"

"You know. She is from the Gautier family north of us."

"I do not know a Margarite. I know Gautier's have alot of kids."

Joe seldom stopped eating to talk, but replied, "Oh, that is Rita."

Elisa glared at Joe. "Stop gobbling your food. Hummm? You say it is Rita? All your girlfriends have names, but this one has a pet name? Did not know you two were acquainted."

Pete grinned his thirty-four year old smile that still retained its impish, youthful charm. "Now Lisa, he can not help it if he has the charms of a Don Juan." Elisa feigned disgust, reminescent of Pete's mom and scoffed, "You men. You are always laughing. Nothing laughable in these times. Now, as I tried to say. Margarite or Rita, whatever the case may be, told me there would be a fair in the village."

"We never get troupes from Paris. How come? Asked Pete.

"According to Lucille. . . .

"Who?" Asked Pete.

"Bartholomew Vervin's wife, she said Paris has become so dangerous circuses and troupes are preferring to go to the villages."

"Hey, now. When is it going to be?" Elisa was pleased to have caught Pete's interest. "Day after tomorrow."

"Want to see the acrobat in his tight tights, eh mom.?" Pete choked over Joe's remark, sputtered and sprayed his mouthful of soup over the table. Elisa rose to get a cloth before reprimanding him. "You are at it again, laughing over things that are not a bit funny." She stalked off and returned with a sloppy, wet rag and flopped it across Pete's mouth. "Need a bib? You men are not laughing? I thought that was funny." She primly seated herself. "I want to go to the fair. Yes, and see the acrobats, tightrope walker, trained dogs, and those stilt-walkers. It is all so entertaining. By the way, Joe, where did you meet Rita?"

"We will find a way to go. We will go." Said Pete as he wiped his face and hid his grin behind his kerchief.

"I met her . . ."

"This is Rita you speak of? Not Mona, Emily, or Amy?"

"Now, mom. I met Rita in the village, at Mr. Bouteau's tobacco shop buying tobacco."

"For herself?"

"No, for her dad and brothers." Elisa shook her head in disdain. "A family of smokers." Abruptly her eyes lit up. She pointed her finger at Joe. "That is where you got the idea to smoke that dirty pipe."

"You are wrong, mom. Remember, grandpere smokes. So does dad. You know I have been working at the tobacco shop, saving for the seed drill Jethro Tull invented. It was the aroma in the shop that tempted me."

Elisa rose to remove the soup kettle. "Mom, let me carry it." As Joe carried the kettle away, Pete whispered in Elisa's ear, "Lisa, you know he pays for his own tobacco."

"Well, if you ask me, he grew up too fast."

The men went outside to the stump that held the anvil, picked up their scythes and headed for the field. "S'pose you best postpone hunting tomorrow and get the field swathed." Joe looked at Pete in surprise. He wanted to go hunting; doing what he wanted, was Joe's tendency. He consoled himself with the thought he could spend all day and still not scar up a rabbit.

"Gotta get the wheat in and grain sacked. You know, son, I remember when mom used to share giggling fits with my mother. She really misses Marie. I want to take her to the fair, where she can laugh and be among other women."

"Definitely, dad. I do not know how many times she has looked at those plates, only to say, 'You know these were mom's.'"

Pete nodded. "I miss my mother, but then I have dad and your company."

It was Daniel, Joe's great grandfather, who had shared his hobby of whittling with Joe. Joe developed the art of carpentry at an early age and was skilled at the craft. At fourteen he had built a four-wheeled wooden cart that replaced their old wobbily two-wheeled cart. He had crafted a table and chairs, as well as a couple of cabinets.

Elisa awakened early to prepare for the village trip. Andy, with his bad leg, did not feel up to lengthy activity and chose to stay home. When all was ready, she gingerly stepped into the cart. "Joe, you do not know how much I enjoy getting into this cart. Your idea of a bench was fantastic. I remember the old cart. You not only had to stand, but also had to be in a certain spot, least it tipped."

"Mom, that was in the old days. Want to give you as many pleasures today, as possible. I am going to the stable and help dad with the ox and yoke."

"Everything going all right?"

"Yes. Thought I would give the animals food before we take off." Joe pulled a draw-stringed bag from his pocket. "Here dad, please take it and buy mom something nice."

"No son, can not do that."

"Please dad. I do not pay any taille."

"Do this for me, please? This bit will not delay the seed drill. I figure we will have it by seedtime."

"Why not buy it, yourself?"

"I am not going to the fair."

"What? Disappoint your mother?"

"I will keep grandpere company, besides, I think mom would enjoy some romance and privacy with you. We have been so busy with harvest. She has been alone alot."

"Think you are right, son. But you will have to tell her yourself."

"What will you be doing today?"

"Grandpere and I are going to the woods and locate walnut. I will want it for a project to surprise mom. I will go tell mom, now." As Joe walked from the stable, he heard his dad merrily whistling while the ox and cow chewed cud. Joe paused to listen to the melodic notes and knew the trip was also good for dad.

"I have been sitting here waiting. Where is Pete?" Asked Elisa.

"Waiting for the animals to finish eating."

She tipped herself sidewise to better see Joe. "Oh, yes. It will be a long day for them. Guess, I am getting impulsive like you."

"Another thing, mom. I am not going."

"Not going? You know how I have looked forward to this."

"Well, grandpere and I have a plan to work on. One that will save you some cleaning time."

Flattered at her son's concern, she asked coyly. "How can you do that? You should not keep secrets from your mother."

"Here he comes." Elisa said in anticipation, scooted around girlishly on the bench and straightened the folds in her dress. "You whistling tunes to that old ox?"

Pete bowed, tipped his feathered hat, and looked up into her face. "No, my fair damsel. I am destined to embark on kidnapping the maiden of my dreams, carting her off for fun and frolic. I whistle from delight. May I boldly inquire? Where hast thou obtained such a beautiful dress, my lady?"

"Will you stop that, and get going?" Joe yoked the ox and cow as Pete stepped into the cart beside his lady. As the wheels rolled down the road, Joe thought of his own escapades and wondered, if womanizing was inherent?

They rode silently for a kilometer, absorbed in thought. "Lisa, you know what this reminds me of?" She turned her bonneted head slowly, "Not really."

"The time we walked hand-in-hand down the path. Remember?"

"Not really. That was with my keeper of the path." Together they laughed and squeezed each other's hand. As they released their hands, Pete, in an affectionate gesture, brought her hand to his mouth, kissed it and laid it upon her lap. "Your hand smells of roses."

Elisa's eyes moistened as she spoke, "Yes. It is a secret of your mother's that she shared with me. It is from pressed flowers gathered in the woods. She showed me how to mix and boil until it was a smooth lotion. She shared that with me, she did."

"That solves the mystery of your perfume. Where did your dress come from?"

Elisa did not answer quickly. "Remember when your mother died? I felt so bad. When both she and Marie were gone, I felt so alone. You, Andy, and Joe were out of the house working hard, venting your sorrow in work. I did what my mother did, weaved and weaved on the loom. Made this dress and put it aside. It would take a special occasion for me to wear it."

"I am honored you chose this day. Mom loved you very much."

"I told her how happy I was to finally have a mother." Elisa looked up into the sky and lowered her head. "I have not found the opportunity to tell dad, that he is the father I never had." Pete reached over and patted her knee, "He knows. He knows."

"Listen. I can hear the celebration. Gaiety is simply marvelous?"

"Just around this turn you can see the village."

"Oh, look at all the booths. Course we can not buy anything, but I must look. Over there, Pete. Look at the acrobat on the high wire. What a long pole he carries. Over there. There. See, those people sitting on bleechers. Must be a wonderful puppet show. Let us see it first. Pete, look at the lady with the cone hat and sash, she is no peasant. All the people. Just look at the crowd." Elisa looked and stopped to view everything. Pete realized it had been a long time since he had seen his Lisa so excited and happy.

"You like this music box?" She turned it around in her hands, viewing the carved lid and sides. Upon opening it, she gasped, "It is playing a part from The Magic Flute? Remember? How magical are memories."

"I will buy it for you." Elisa stared at him in amazement and stammered, "You have money for this?"

"Yes."

"No, I do not want it. You know our money should go for food."

Pete shook his head, "Not this money. It is marked for you."

"For me? For my desires?

"Of course."

"I would rather spend it elsewhere." Elisa took his arm and guided him to another booth. "I saw something we would both like over at that booth." She pointed to a tented stall with brightly colored banners flapping in the wind.

"What is over there, Lisa?"

"Wonderful things." The crowd shifted and Pete could see the display. "Why it is a bunch of Toby jugs. You want a jug? Elisa squeezed his arm and nudged closer to him. "Let us buy Joe a Toby mug." Pete pointed his finger and asked the vendor, "We will take the Toby mug over there. The one with the squire."

"Lisa, you wait here while he packages the Toby. I want to take a peek at the archery contest and be back in a few minutes." Pete left and sneaked over to the booth and bought the music box. After hiding it in his pocket, he returned to the booth where Elisa was waiting. "Lisa, it is getting near sunset. You ready to go?"

"Yes. It has been a wonderful day." Pete started to help her into the cart and reached for the Toby jug she cradled in her hands, "I will put it in the back of the cart."

"Oh, no. I am carrying this home. We will surprise Joe after supper."

"Fine idea." Pete poked the ox with the goad. They turned from the Paris road into the road leading to home. The windows were aglow with light. "He is at it again."

"Lisa, what do you mean?"

"Burning so many of my candles. I have told him we need to go sparingly with them."

"Probably reading, like Daniel did. You remember?"

"Well, I would say dad is as guilty." Added Elisa.

"Like dad? Joe is worse. Dad shares his reading by speaking about it. Joe's nose is stuck in a book every moment he isn't working."

Pete opened the upper half of the door and while struggling to open the lower, Elisa peered into the room. There sat Joe in his rocker with books piled around within easy reach. She saw the number of candlesticks nearby holding burning candles. "What have I told you about using so many candles? Besides, you are liable to start a fire among those books and papers." Joe sheepishly looked at his mom from the corner of his eye. "Sorry, mom, did not think you would be home until later. Would you like me to replace that half door with a full one?"

"No." Elisa snapped.

Joe quickly lowered his nose into his book awaiting her reprimand. It still worked with mom--tell the truth and repercussions were few, sometimes nil. So different from his dad's stoic judgment that seemed immune to any of his influences.

Pete asked. "Is dad resting?"

"Yes. We did a lot of walking in the woods. Think his leg began to bother him. Mom, did you enjoy the fair?"

"Oh, my yes. It was so exciting. I get excited talking about it. Tell you about it after supper. Can not keep my mind on cooking, if I get to talking."

Pete winked at Joe. Out of the corner of her eye, Elisa saw the wink. "Pete, will you stir the kettle and put it on the table?"

"Joe, go wake your grandpere."

"Lisa, you planning on doing something?" Pete asked.

"Change my dress."

"Why change from that pretty? Keep it on until bedtime."

Elisa feigned an extremely bewildered look and asked, "You think I would risk you spitting soup all over it?" She hastened to the bedroom before her gigles could be heard. Returning, she picked up a loaf of bread from the cabinet and placed it on the table. The family was too hungry and worn out to interrupted supper with talking. When everyone had finished the meal, Elisa asked, "Joe will you hang the kettle back in the hearth?" She slipped over to the cabinet, removed the Toby jug and set it at Joe's place.

"What is this?"

"Unwrap it carefully." Joe removed the first layer of paper. "Gotta save this. It is an issue of the Rambler. Oh, so is this second layer." Then he paused. "A Toby. A Toby just like the one I had. Merci. Tell me, how was your day?"

"Of course, the social affair was led by the mayor, Pierre Montmorin and Francois Bonet, our blacksmith; with help from Mike Slagger and Karl Brener. I am sure the whole village was at the Yule Feast celebrating Plough Monday. There was so much. Can not remember it all. There were flais, corn dollies and the last sheaf of harvest. The carnival was funny. It mimicked King Louis' court. We elected king, queen and courtiers and when they put on the masques, the crowd roared in laughter. So funny. Then they exaggerated an imitation of the royal minuette and a courtly feast. Everyone was laughing until tears rolled down their faces. I watched this, while Pete watched the young men play football, archery, wrestling and fighting with wooden staves."

"Son, you should have entered the archery contest."

Elisa and Pete had been sleeping, when she nudged Pete to awaken him. In a frightened voice, she asked, "What are those noises?" Drowsily, Pete listened. Soon he was wide-awake from the dragging, scraping sounds, and sat up in bed. Then came more pounding noises. Pete recognized the hammering sounds and slide back into bed. "That is Joe. Must be working on one of his projects."

"Ooh, Joe said he had a surprise for me. I am going to peek."

"You will not. If he has a surprise for you, do not spoil it." Pete mumbled drowsily and fell asleep. Elisa laid down in bed. Pete was right. Must not spoil it.

Joe was up with the sunrise. He wanted to see his mom's expression and pleasure over his surprise. Last night he had dragged the split rails and stacked them. Previously he had carefully drawn his plan for the length of the rails and the needed lumber. Each plank had supporting carved braces beneath, which he had firmly attached to the wall. The bookshelves lined the west wall by the fireplace. All books and papers were neatly arranged with rocks serving as bookends. The Toby mug decorated the center shelving. All was ready for his mom's viewing. Andy's footsteps caught Joe's attention.

"Grandpere, what do you think about the cut walnut, now?"

"That is good work, Joe. So useful."

Pete sauntered from the bedroom and stretched. "Slept like a rock, until that racket began. What were you working on?"

"Sorry, dad. Figured you two were so worn out, it would not awaken you. The noise did not last long."

"No, we went back to sleep."

"It awakened mom?"

"Of course. She said something about your secret and wanted to peek."

"Did she?"

"She wanted to. Told her to go back to sleep and she did. What were you making, son?"

"Over there. The bookshelves."

"Brilliant, son. Brilliant. A fine job."

"Shhhh, here she comes." Elisa was wearing the robe she had woven, and immediately spotted the men at the table and joined them.

"You always dress in the morning. What is with this robe? Too curious to dress?" Asked Pete.

"Were you working on my surprise last night?"

"Yes."

"Elisa, where is our tea?" Andy teased.

"My surprise. Suppose it is not done, yet?" Asked Elisa, ignoring Andy.

"Oh, mother dear, but it is. Look at the rocker." She clapped her hands in joy. "You cleaned up the book mess. Where did you put all those books?"

Joe pointed to the wall, "Mom, look past the rocker."

"For heavens sake." She stammered, rose from her chair and walked over to get a better view. She touched the carved braces, "It is absolutely beautiful. You are so clever. So talented." Andy nudged Joe's knee under the table. "Now Elisa, he is conceited enough. Do not add to the problem."

"Where is that tea, Lisa?" Pete teased.

"It changes the looks of the whole room. May I put a vase of flowers on this space?"

"Mom, it is your bookshelf. I made it for you to make your cleaning easier." Elisa returned to the table and bent over the men and embraced both. Tears slipped down her cheeks. "Now, I am going to dress."

"Dad, do women always cry when they are happy?" Asked Joe.

"Think so. Has to do with the extent of their joy. Why?"

"Oh, just wondered. Just wondered. When I am happy, I sure do not feel like bawling." Pete wrapped an arm around him. "Son, there are times men bawl because we are human."

Andy added, "Men with stone souls, don't cry."

"Going to feed the livestock." Said Joe.

"Hey, you do not have to do that on days you work at the tobacco shop." Said Andy.

"Wish I could work more than a day a week. Lean times at the shop." Said Joe.

Pete turned to tell Joe, tonight they must work on a plan to portion out the grain and make it last until seedtime, but Joe had disappeared.

"Joe gone already?" Elisa asked, as she returned with the tea.

"Yes. He can move when he wants to. Are you going to weave today? Last of the fleece is in the west corner of the stable."

"No, I have run out of projects. After the excitement of yesterday, feel like sitting in the rocker and reading."

"Well, why don't you?"

"Joe's books are filled with big words. Thoughts I can not understand."

"Now, Lisa. Not all of them. You remember your German?"

"Why, of course. Speak it whenever I visit Ursala Voiter."

Pete rose from the chair to select a book from the wall shelves. "I think . . . Know I kept every one of dad's books. Here it is." He removed the book and brought it to Elisa, placing it in front of her. "Here. You will enjoy Friedrich Klopstock. It is poetry." Elisa eagerly opened the book, "What have you in mind for today?"

"Well, first. Woman, move to the rocker. I need room on this table for paperwork. Have to rework the grain schedule. I have grain allotted to May. Can not stretch it any further. Was hoping Joe had an idea or two. If we are lucky, the sheep and swine will have new born, but they must be fed."

"You will think of something. You are just like your dad. Ask him."

"Wrong, I do not have his planning insight, and we have already discussed it."

"What have we discussed?" Andy muttered, and limped inside from his morning walk. Elisa continued reading. A big smile spread over her face as she remembered Pete's many plans that proved his statement wrong.

Rita tapped on the paned window of the tobacco store. Joe rushed to usher her inside. "Is Mr. Bouteau gone?"

"You know this is his regular lunch time. We have always met at this time." Rita dropped her head and stared at the floor. Joe touched her chin and raised her head until he could look into her eyes. "You are crying. Did I say something wrong?"

"Let us go to the backroom."

"No. Not when you are crying." Rita walked directly to the backroom with Joe following. "We have got to talk."

"Sure, we will talk." He seated her on Mr. Bouteau's couch. Among the storage boxes, Mr. Bouteau kept a couch for his napping. Joe sat near Rita and wiped her tears with his kerchief. "Why are these beautiful eyes weeping?" Rita burst forth her statement, "I do not feel well. I am pregnant."

"Oh." Joe could not manage anymore words.

"Yes. Instead of this backroom, we should have been visiting our folks. Now . . . Oh, I am so worried."

"Do not fret, sweetheart. All will work out. We have to plan. First we will visit your family and give them the news."

"Oh no, Joe. I will not tell my folks. Dad would thrash you to the bone. I do not want a forced marriage.

"We will not tell either of our parents." Joe added. Rita's eyes opened wide, "We must tell your folks. Must, must, must. I do not want them thinking you were forced into marriage."

"Calm down, my sweet. After work, I will call on you and during our visit, I will ask your dad when you may visit my family." Rita's tears did not stop, but she hesitanted, "He will agree to that. Will your folks kick me out?"

"No. They will be shocked and disappointed in me. They will not take it out on you. We will get married and be blessed with our baby. Now stop crying. You do not want Mr. Bouteau to see your tears. Take your family's tobacco home. I will be at your house about seven."

"Did you have a good lunch, Mr. Bouteau?" Asked Joe.

"Bierocks, my favorite. Can not figure out why they always give me the burns."

"Might be eating, too many." Mr. Bouteau gave a hearty "arf, arf," and added, "If this be the price, so be it."

Joe was pleased about Bouteau's indigestion as it meant he would sleep it off. Joe wanted to be alone with his thoughts while doing the store's inventory. There would not be time to face his parents this evening. Tomorrow, he would tell them. He needed time to think. He did not want to cause pain for Rita's family, shame for his dad, or the ache of disappointment for his mom. Joe's conflicting emotions of happiness and pain shifted within him until he felt his mind numbed from the turmoil.

During the afternoon, Mr. Bouteau had given Joe his requested break to do brief shopping, and he bought a ring from the seed-drill savings. Joe was relieved when the tobacco shop closed. The walk from the village in the fresh air did not clear his mind, and he still had no idea how he should break the news. It must wait. Tonight's visit to Rita's parents and the engagement would be enough of a surprise.

Pete swung his arm in an arched circle over the papers covering the table, "Son, glad you are home. Need your input." Joe put a hand on one pile of papers. "What is this litter?"

"Your dad is working out a plan to stretch the grain until harvest."

"And need your help." Pete added.

"Not tonight. Will get with you later." Pete looked at Elisa, bewildered. Joe had never before refused to help him.

"I am going to marry Rita. I am visiting her family this evening to ask for her hand."

Elisa slumped into the nearest chair. "When did this happen?"

"I am older than dad, when he married."

"Son, that is not the point. Your mom means, you have the cart before the ox. The girl visits the boy's family first. You have not had her to our house. We know of her, but we have not met her."

"She is coming to visit tomorrow night. I have to get ready and leave." Joe hurried to the bedroom. He dreaded their stunned silence. Would he be able to leave without much adieu?

At first, Joe could not knock at the Gautier door. He paused, took a deep breath and knocked.

"Welcome to our home, young man, I am Michael Gautier. You are Peter de Regnier's, son."

"That is right, sir, Joseph. At the moment he entered, children scampered towards a wall and stood in line, staring at him. Joe felt conspicuous.

"Do not let the little one's spook you. So many, we have them line-up. It makes introductions easier." Joe, relaxed. He liked Mr. Gautier's laughter and wit. "This is my wife, Diane. She is holding Teresa. Then here is Joseph, Bernadette . . ."

"I am three." She smiled up at Joe. Joe tapped her under the chin.

"This here is Louis, Catherine, Charles, James, Paul, and you know Rita." Suddenly the children broke line and ran in different directions, to settled on their previous activities.

"We have two older ones. My son, Jacque, he farms the plot north of us. Maria is married and has two children. They live in Louvier."

"Merci. You have walked quiet a distance, Joe. Would you men like some cheese and crackers?" Asked Diane.

"Yes, Diane, that would be nice. Would you bring us a bottle from the cabinet? What is this call about?"

"I am calling on Rita. We have visited when she was at the tobacco shop, and become friends."

Rita said proudly. "Daddy makes his own wine." Joe quickly asked, "You have grapevines?"

"You bet. They are hidden in the woods." Joe began to feel Mike was no longer a stranger, but another man with clever plans.

"Have woods on the north, south, and west sides of the farm, but east is mostly farmland. A large farm needs lots of kids. Will cut you some grapevine rootings around seedtime, if you would like."

"Sure would."

"Rita, come over and sit by your dad. You came courting my daughter?"

Joe stiffened, sat erect, and answered. "Yes sir, I . . . , I'd . . . , I would like to ask you for Rita's hand."

"Rita, do you love, Joe"

"Oh, I do, daddy."

"Then you have my permission to marry. Let us sip our wine and play some whist."

"Wait a minute." Said Joe, as he stood and bent over the table to grasp Rita's hand, "Will you marry me?"

"Yes, my bouquiner." Joe slide the ring on her finger.

Joe welcomed the long walk home. Time to think. Time to plan. Tonight only good things had mattered. The evening visit had been exhilerating. How wonderful to have so many brothers and sisters; and it put magic into their home. Now, they were his in-laws. How wonderful to plant grapevines in the woods and make wine. To be accepted. To win Rita. To love and be loved.

In the morning Joe arose before sunrise to review dad's drafted plans. He lit a candle and as he had hoped, the papers still lay on the table. Quietly, he stacked the scattered papers together and sat in the rocker to study each drawn chart. The last chart showed livestock grain allotments reaching to May, which left a shortage of three months. That gave him an idea. He pushed the doors wide open and lit the hearth to boil water for tea and let his idea further brew. After finishing his second cup of tea, he had developed a solution. He placed the papers neatly on the table and left to feed livestock.

"I see Joe has been at my papers." Pete grumbled as he and Elisa headed for the table.

"He has tea ready. Wonderful, I will get an early start on cleaning. You know Rita is coming this evening."

"Humph, appears he is trying to sweeten us up." Pete sat at the table, waiting for Elisa to bring the tea and seat herself. "I hear him in the stable feeding stock." He muttered, still ruffled from last night's rebuff. "Young love turns brains into mush. Probably can not concentrate on a plan." Elisa extended her hand to Pete, "Here, put some sugar in your mouth, you sour old goat."

"Getting yourself all elated about the marriage, eh girlie?"

"Pete, you know I do not like to be called girlie. Something is bothering you. Spit it out."

"Worry. Worrying about feeding us and keeping the livestock alive. Famine everywhere. Conditions are not getting better. Only worse."

"What is getting worse?" Joe asked as he entered the room and set a hand-rake against the door. Pete turned, swung an arm towards the door, and bellowed, "Put that rake in the stable or outside. Mom's cleaning today."

"Pete. You do not have to growl at him. You have been nothing but an old grouch since starting that grain plan."

"What is the commotion about so early in the morning?" Andy asked.

Joe seldom saw dad so annoyed. What was so important? He knew grandpere had a temper, his great grandpere had had the same hot temper over monarchism, but dad was fuming over grain. Survival, that was it. Truly, both dad and grandpere turned into hotheads when it came to matters of survival.

"Think I have a plan, dad."

Joe's statement immediately snapped Pete out of his stubborn, sulking mood. "What is that? What did you say, Joe?" Joe sighed, he had captured his dad's attention. "Got a plan."

"Sit down, let us hear it, son." Pete patted the table with both hands, excitement gleamed from his eyes and a broad grin spread across his face, expressing impish anticipation.

"That can wait. I have heard enough about that grain plan." Said Elisa, still angry over Pete's behavior, she stood firm. "First, I am pouring us more tea. Then we will peacefully listen to Joe's account of his visit with Rita's family." Pete realized he had placed his concerns above Joe's engagement. He looked wistfully up into Elisa's face as she poured tea and said softly, "Tea's quite tasty."

Elisa sat with folded hands upon the table. "Now, Joe. Tell us about the Gautier family. Am ever so anxious to hear."

"I really enjoyed the whole family. Wished I had brought my pipe. Three of the boys and Mike, smoke. Her mother's name is Diane. It was so funny, dad. I walked into their house; it is like ours, but larger and had all these doors leading to small sleeping rooms. Then these kids came pouring out of the rooms, scampering to a wall like spilled marbles and lined themselves against a wall and stood looking at me."

"What?" Questioned Pete. Joe chuckled a bit. "It is Mike's way of introducing his family." Pete scratched his head, "Knew he had a lot of kids. I have seen them at church and they take an entire church pew." Elisa eagerly bent over the table towards Joe, "Go on."

"Mike did not waste much time asking me about my intentions. He told Rita to join us at the table and I put the ring on her finger. It was a wonderful evening."

"Ring?" Pete asked.

Joe faced his dad to reply, "Yes. I bought a ring from my seed-drill savings." Pete smiled and reached to shake Joe's hand. "Shows responsibility. I am proud of you son." Joe had burning feelings of self-anguish and knew it was time to tell the other side of his news. "No dad. I have let you, mom, grandpere, and Rita down."

"How is that son?"

Joe found strength in thinking of Rita, and faced his dad. "Rita's pregnant."

"What?" Roared Pete. Elisa spilled her tea. Silently, Andy took his kerchief and wiped up the spill. Pete slapped his hand on the table, shouting, "You go to her house. To her family and wallow in Mike's respect and did not tell him? You go there immediately and tell Mike. Face your come-up-pence. Shame. Shameful of you, son."

"Give the boy a chance to speak." Said Andy, as he slide his hand under the table and took hold of Joe's.

"Dad, Rita did not want me to tell her parents. Begged me not to tell. Said her dad would thrash me, and she did not want him forcing our marriage. Dad, she cried and cried until I promised not to tell."

"Then, why the hell did you tell us?"

"She insisted. She did not want mom, or you, to feel she had forced me into marriage."

"Poor child." Muttered Elisa.

Joe felt dad's criticism comforting. He did not know why, but now found it easier to unfold the details. His nausea was gone. "Rita's eighteen, mom."

"Does not matter. It is a male's responsibility to protect his affair de coeur." Pete added.

Joe nodded his head, "I realize that, dad."

Pete glared at Joe, "Seems your realization comes a bit late."

Joe looked at his mother, her elbows bent in support of her bowed head. Cupped hands hid her face. "Mom, do not cry." Joe pleaded. She removed her hands. "I am not crying, just thinking about the poor child and what she is enduring. What month is she in?"

Joe squirmed as he replied, "The first. Please do not be mad at us, mom."

Elisa, rose and leaned across the table facing Joe. "I am not going to say another word until you promise me Rita and you will go to church tomorrow and pray together."

"We planned to mom, and also arrange for bans. Then we can set a wedding date." Elisa's troubled expression disappeared. "When will you bring Rita?"

"She told me, after supper."

"I will have no such thing. You go over there early and bring her for supper. Show Rita's family we are as cordial as they."

Joe felt relief from spitting out his torment and words came out in whispered tones. "I will. I will."

"Best, you hitch the ox and go in the cart."

"Merci, dad." Joe humbly answered, and felt happiness again resurge within him. Andy leaned over to Pete and whispered, "the grain plan?"

Pete slapped his hand on the table, catching Elisa and Joe in startled attention. "Now, son. What is the plan you spoke of?" Elisa stood and tossed her arms in mid-air, "You men talk. I am going to start cleaning. Want to bake something special for tonight."

"Well, son, what is it?"

"It has to do with you grandpere, and our walks together in the woods. I remember one time when we were sitting on rocks and you held a red Welsh poppy. You gazed at it as you told me about the beauty of the woods and how it fulfilled so many needs."

"Yes, Joe, I remember." Said Andy with dewey eyes.

"You talked about a Swiss naturalist who had written a book on the fauna of Switzerland and transhumance."

"What?" Asked Pete.

"That is the word. Grandpere, you would not let me leave the woods until I had memorized the dang thing, and could spell it backwards. I will never forget it."

Andy chuckled, and said, "Pete, the word means pastoral nomadism, where you move livestock each season between mountain summer-pasture and lower winter-fields. Or between wet and dry seasonal grazing land."

"Dad, instead of feeding our livestock during March, April, and May, we can graze them in the woods during those months. Then our grain should last until harvest."

"Think you have something." Pete uttered, heaved a sigh and leaned back in his chair. "You did it son. I am proud of you. Joy and excitement seized Joe and words spilled from his mouth. "Dad. I will split rails, make posts to sink into the earth. Some places the trees can serve as posts. Different areas, I will enclose railing posts to keep stock from roaming. Course, it will take time, as we will have to lead our stock back and forth."

"We should be so lucky." Said Pete as he smiled at Andy and patted Joe on the back. Pete looked around and saw Elisa whisking the floor in the sleeping room. "Joe, one more thing. Do not want to worry your mother, but would you crawl through the tunnel soon, and check if it is intact. Last time I checked, there was a nest of woodchucks living in it."

"Sure will, but the war is over. Why would we be using it?"

CHAPTER 11: WEAVER OF WISHES

Monty and Teresa had eaten their supper rolls, and Monty's anger grew as the captain ordered them down into steerage. He vowed to confront the captain the next evening and refuse to enter steerage. "Teresa, keep your mouth shut, while in this pit. Do not talk. Hard telling what diseases you could get from inhaling through your mouth." Down they went, into the pit of writhing humanity and asphyxiating air reeking from toxic fumes of ammonia sewage.

Standing next to Teresa, he no longer felt alone. Feelings of protecting her rose within him. Would her frail body withstand the rigors of the trip? He had finished the story of Joe and Rita's love, and fell asleep dreaming of love.

A coughing seizure from the man next to him, awakened Monty. The man was unable to control the spasm and sank to the floor. Monty struggled in the crowded conditions to bend and pick up the man. It was useless. The man was dead.

Monty felt his heartbeat quicken in agony. He must concentrate on something other than the dead man at his feet. He needed to substitute moments of joy and happiness to his dismal situation; something far away from this reality. He remembered the story of Elisa, the weaver of wishes. He had been dreaming about love, and again closed his eyes for the lulling affects of recollection to sweep him into slumber's dreamland.

"Son, about using the tunnel, there is cause to be prepared, even though Turgot has been dismissed and Necker appointed. I heard visitors to our village, and villagers themselves, speak of seeing starving masses in Paris, as well as the miners from up north. Taille is constantly being increased. Taxes and hunger are driving a few to mad violence. Heard, one old man was killed in a Paris street for his shoes. Where all this dissent will lead, I do not know. Can not be too careful, things are getting worse. When you have to watch what you say and what you do, that is fear. Fear is a monster and can erupt from any direction. Which reminds me, you best, not plan on any wedding celebration in Paris."

"I will not. Will check the tunnel soon."

"Do it without your mom knowing, eh?"

"Sure dad. Think I will go to the woods now to scrounge and pick up fallen grain from the ground. I noticed wild animals shake off grain while foraging in and around our crops."

Elisa came walking into the room, shaking a rag in mid-air. "Joe, on your way back, pick some flowers for the table. All the flowers can not be dried up."

"I will try to find some. Where are the sacks?" Asked Joe. Pete shifted from his brooding thoughts.

"I have moved the sacks outside. They are hanging on a spike by the rock pile."

Andy had gotten ready to go outside, took a sack and his cane, "Wait Joe, I am coming, too."

"Woman, leave my papers alone." Elisa replied, in words synchronized with every swish of her dust-rag, "I am supposed to clean with your papers here, boots over there, Sunday hat still on the mantel?" Elisa's spirited bursts of vigor pleased Pete, he pointed and asked, "Lisa, who left that in the rocker?"

"Oh, I meant to put the book on the shelf." She quickly grabbed it.

"Guess, I will get a sack, too, and see what grain I can salvage from the field." Pete carried his hat and papers to the bedroom and returned to put on work-boots. Elisa was singing an old German folk song.

"A-ha, what Meistersinger doth grace our humble abode?" Elisa stopped sweeping and raised the broom, waving it at Pete. "Get to work." Pete hastily skipped out the door to join Joe and Andy.

Elisa's thoughts dwelled on the future. She would have a daughter and female company so lacking since Marie's death. She would have a grandchild. She had hungered so long for more children. Now all could be.

The sun was about to set when Pete and Andy walked through the door. "Lisa, something smells good. What have you been making?"

"I tried to work out something. I took a bit of broth from the kettle, bits of lamb jerky, a potato, plus a few other things to make a meat pie. Hope it is good."

"The smell guarantees it." Pete pulled the chair from the table to sit. "My, my, ain't everything spiffy and fancy. You want, I should wear my Sunday hat?"

"You silly Frenchman. Do not knock my vase over and spill water on my cloth."

"Where did this cloth come from. Have not seen it?"

"One I wove last winter, wishing for a special occasion." Pete looked at her adoringly, "My darling weaver of wishes."

Joe loudly kicked at the door. "Didn't think you would find that much grain." Said Pete. Joe heaved two partially filled sacks from his shoulders and sat them on the floor. He laid a bouquet of bittersweet on a nearby stool. "Appears it will make all of a bag and a half."

"With my half-sack of grain dad, and what grandpere found in the north field, we will have two bags. Sure help our grain allotments. Hey, mom, what is that delicious smell?" Elisa kept right on with her cooking, but replied, "Wait and see."

"I found you some bittersweet. There it is on the stool."

"I must put it in my vase."

"What are you baking?"

"Joe, you will be late in picking up Rita.

"No, Mr. Gautier said he would drop her off on his way to deliver a couple bottles of wine for Jacque.

"That is nice." Elisa reached for the laver, a bronze water vessel with two spouts. The storage jar of tea stood on the crossbeams alongside other crockery. "Think I will place the tea on the chest. Was that a knock on the door? There it is again."

"It is Rita." Joe dashed over to open the door. Pete followed Joe, "Want to have some words with Mike." Pete returned as Joe was introducing Rita. "You know my mom, Elisa. This is my dad, Pete, and my grandpere. Lambert Andre. We call him Andy. Please sit here." Joe adjusted the chair and Elisa carried the meat pie to the table. Pete was amazed at Rita's beauty. "You look very lovely, tonight."

"Thank you, Mr. Regnier."

"Dad, you are making her shy."

"Mrs. Regnier, your home astounds me. It is so different."

"In what way?"

Rita looked over one shoulder and then the other. "It is so quiet. At home we have to step over things, even kids. And those shelves over there. Why I have never seen such beautiful shelves and so many books. The Bible is the only book in our house. Have you read all those books, Joe?"

"Most of them."

"I learned script and letters. I can only read parts of the Bible. "What is that little book on the end?"

"That is grandpere's Aldus Manutius grammar. Books on the

lower shelf are Greek and Latin classics. Also, Chaucer's Canterbury Tales. They are on the bottom shelf because only grandpere reads those."

"Mr. Regnier, tell me about this pretty home. Did you build it?"

"No, my child. The original hearth has been here through generations. Additions were made throughout the years. But my dad and I did put up the dividing wall in the sleeping room. Andy said his grandpere's dad helped build the first sleeping room. The framework was formed by crucks, curved timber beams placed in facing pairs, with tops meeting, and lashed together with cord. The roof is thatch of reeds. These walls are of wattle, intertwined twigs, reinforced with clay and mud daubbing. Which reminds me. Joe, we need to chauk before long."

"Rita, you will soon be another Mrs. Regnier. Please call us mom and dad."

"Mom, Rita thinks we should go to America after we are married." Elisa pushed her plate away and sank back into her chair. "What? I have never heard of such a thing. Why in the world?"

"She thinks it would be better. You know, after the baby comes, gossip and the wrath of her dad. Besides, she thought you would kick us out." Said Joe.

"You will do no such thing." Pete ordered, "This is your land. Your home. Rita, you will soon be our family and your dad, Michael, can just stew--if he so chooses."

Andy said, "Rita, once your dad sees your baby, believe me, he will change. Babies bring their own magic. Do not fret, early births are quite common."

"Rita, please change your mind." Elisa begged. Rita began weeping. Pete ignored the sobbing. "Enough of this foolish talk. Food is getting cold. Let us finish our meal. By the way, Rita, I told your dad you kids would be bundling tonight." Joe looked at Rita longingly. "Tomorrow morning, we will take the path to the church to set bans." At mention of the path, Elisa and Pete exchanged nostalgic glances. Rita wiped her tears away. "Mom, do you think we will be able to set an early date?" Elisa felt her heart skip a beat. Her daughter had called her mom. "Let us plan that way. There is much to do. What would you like?"

"I was feeling guilt-ridden over my parent's plans. Now, I am grateful and excited. My mom and dad are planning a barn dance. Dad has been selecting his best wines. Mom is fussing over her kraut and making special crackers and breads. Dad said he might even try brewing some kvas from fermented black rye bread. His mother came from Russia. It is a powerful Russian drink."

"You did not tell me about this?"

"I was having inner turmoil over disappointing my folks. I could not talk about it."

"It will be a gala affair. Lisa, best you get the special dress out, again." Said Pete.

Andy said, "I can not wait to sample the kvas."

Joe and Rita's marriage was the last celebration for families and neighbors before the elements of winter struck. Pete taught Joe the making of the mixture for mudding the house. The grain plan had successfully been completed. The men split rails in preparation for the spring construction of the extra room. Elisa taught Rita to weave as they chatted, giggled and wove baby clothing. Andy began giving Rita reading lessons.

As Christmas time neared, the house filled with whispers, giggles and secretive actions. One evening they set up the creche. Each family member was working on their gifts. Pete had taken the burned cradle from its hiding place and was rebuilding it for Rita. Andy was carving. Rita was weaving a blouse for Elisa. Elisa was making extra candles for Pete. Joe was bottling ink made from lampblack and linseed oil for Pete. Pine boughs lay upon the mantel and some were burning in the fireplace. The odor drifted throughout the room.

"Should I pluck this goose in the stable?"

Elisa nodded and added, "Joe, now save those feathers, need to make a pillow for the baby."

"Mom, I have added the dried currants to the pudding. What now?" Asked Rita.

"Give it twenty stirs and pour into this pot for baking." Elisa answered, as she removed crockery from a shelf. "I do know how to bake a goose." Rita said proudly, anxiously awaiting Andy's return with the bird.

"Wonderful, child. But first, let us work on stuffing this fish."

"What is it?"

"It is tench. Early this morning, after Joe brought in the pine boughs, he went ice fishing in the brook. He wanted a pike, but caught this instead. Fixed right, it is pretty tasty. When done, we will pack it in snow. We must be sure to finish the goose for tonight. You know Reveillon is supposed to be the greatest meal of the year. We can sing Joy to the World as we leave from Christmas Mass and come home for Reveillon."

"Let me watch you fix the fish. I want to know how to make it."

On New Year's day, Joe, Andy, and Pete were the first ones up and greeted everyone with, "bonne annee." Joe started tea and Pete started a fire in the fireplace. "My word, you men are up early." Elisa began breakfast. Rita walked into the room, "Oh, these men, mom. Probably too eager to open their presents. Still little boys at heart."

"I am sure hungry this morning. Men must be too. They rise before me, make tea and tend to the fire." When all had finished eating, Pete and Joe decided to play along with the 'little boys' remark. They grabbed plates and skipped gleefully as they cleared the table, chanting, "gift time, gift time." Andy, seated in his rocker, happily tapped out a beat with his cane and enjoyed the frolic.

"Well, I have never seen such likings." Said Elisa. Rita stared, she had never seen Pete and Joe comically cavorting. Pete pulled one chair away from the table and pointed to the lone chair. "This is the gift-chair." Joe reached for a pillow and tossed it into the gift-chair.

"Now, who shall be first?"

"No volunteers? You first mom." Joe guided her to the chair.

"Everyone get their present for mom, from your hiding place and put the gift on the table."

"This is fun." Rita exclaimed, as she and the men went in differenct directions and returned to place gifts on the table. Andy reached beneath his rocker and placed a small package on the table.

Elisa opened the nearest gift, it was Rita's. "Child, you have done beautiful work on this blouse. Then Elisa opened the small box and stared at its contents. "What is it? Take it from the box so we can see." Pete grumbled. An intricately carved, wooden flower pendant hung on a leather thong.

"Merci, thank you Andy."

Pete pushed another box towards her. Elisa had the wrapper loose when she recognized the gift and began crying, "Pete, you bought the music box at the fair. She opened the lid and out came the strains from The Magic Flute.

"Now, close your eyes, mom, while I get your present. I could not put it on the table. You can open your eyes now. You are now reading, I made this for you." Elisa gawked at the carved rocker.

"You have anything to say?" Asked Pete. Elisa rose, walked over and sat in her rocker. "I am speechless."

"Mom, you can not sit there all night. We are giving gifts, you know." Said Joe.

"Your turn, Rita." Joe said, and seated her in the gift-chair. Mom rose and rushed to the sleeping room and came back with her gift, "You men just standing there. Where are your gifts?"

"Never mind. Open your present, Rita." She tore into the wrapping. "A dress. I was getting worried as I am growing so big. Oh, here is an apron, too." She jumped from the chair to give Elisa a hug and kiss.

"Who said you could leave the chair?" Asked Pete, and Rita dutifully sat down. Joe had his herchief and blindfolded Rita. "What are you doing, Joe?"

"You will peek, you are so ornery." Pete left for the stable and returned with the cradle. Elisa gasped so loudly Rita asked, "What's wrong, mom?"

"Nothing, my dear."

"Now, you can take the blindfold off ." Rita's mouth opened, she slapped her cheeks and tears flowed as she viewed the cradle. Then Elisa's sniffles increased until she too, was again weeping. "Dad rebuilt it for you. Is this supposed to be joy? Rita, you can bawl into this blindfold." He retied it around her head and left for the stable to return with a rocking chair. Elisa let out another loud gasp.

"Now, Mom." Joe said, as he looked at her in a mockish peeve. "Rita, I am so proud you have been learning to read." He jerked the blindfold away. Rita stared, momentarily speechless, and asked, "My own rocker?"

"That is right. One you can rock and read to our baby. "Good grief, dad, they are at it again. You and I better go for a walk, while the ladies bawl."

"Not so fast son. You best set yourself in the chair. Must we blindfold you?"

"I will behave." Again feet shuffled into scattered areas and Andy retrieved his package. Three gifts were on the table. "Open my first, Joe, it is this one." Said Rita.

"The special tabacco brand I always wanted. But my pipe makes you sick."

"It will not after a few more months." Joe reached for the larger package on the table. "Now this feels like a book." Elisa whispered to Rita, "He has been interested in stars since he was three."

"Mom, how did you know I have wanted a copy of On the Revolutions of Heavonly Bodies ever since Copernicus died. Merci." Placing the book in his lap, he reached for the small package Andy laid upon the table. "A pipe, and the fanciest one I have ever seen. Merci, dear grandpere." He saw an envelope with glued seeds sprinkled on the front. "This is from you, dad? What can it be?" Joe opened the flap and pulled out the slip of paper. He said nothing and stared in awe at the paper. Suddenly, up he sprang, toppling his chair to the floor and raising the paper slip high in the air as he danced around. He grabbed Rita and swung her in circles.

"What is it, Joe?"

"It is a paid receipt for the seed-drill."

"Now, it is your turn, Dad."

Pete answered, "No. It is dad's turn. Make him get out of the rocker so we can see what he has hidden beneath it." Andy limped over and sat in the gift chair. Everyone disappeared and returned placing gifts on the table.

"Which should I open first?"

"This one," said Elisa as she pushed the knitted sweater towards him. Andy opened his presents and found the sweater, a fleece-lined cap from Joe, and a fleece-lined jacket from Pete.

"Aha. This must be from you, Rita." Andy glowed and stroked the bottle of Kvas.

Joe said, "Now, it has to be your turn, dad. Sit."

"Not so fast, son. I bet dad's got something hidden under his rocker." Pete went over and reached under the rocker and found nothing.

"Ha. Fooled you." Andy then hobbled to the bookshelf and came back to put a large package on the table. He had made Pete a boardgame, a backgammon with twenty squares carved from Joe's leftover walnut. Pete began opening the gift closest to him. "Who is this from?"

"Me, dad," said Rita. Inside were a pair of knitted mittins and scarf with his initials sewn in the corner. Pete inspected them saying, "Too nice, merci."

"Here is another." He reached for the larger, rolled bundle. "What is this?"

"I wove a shawl for your shoulders to wear while you read." Said Elisa.

"How about a walk, son? Could use a bit of fresh air. Pine boughs are making my eyes tear." Said Pete.

"Not yet, dad. Here is a bottle of ink for your plans you make." Then Joe drug out a beautifully carved, standing rack from beneath the table. "I made this to put next to your rocker to hold your Ramblers."

"Bless you, son. Now, how about that walk?"

CHAPTER 12: RAGING SEA

The steerage door was opened and Monty awakened to the blessed dawn. Teresa and Monty had finished the breakfast line-up when they noticed officers carrying a body from steerage onto the deck. Monty was relieved they had found the man. However, the officers returned with another body and still another two bodies. Monty's sea-sickness was over, but he vomited nevertheless. Immigrants gathered around the captain as he said a few prayers over the bodies that were cast overboard. Monty wondered how many more funerals, before the trip would end.

"Am sure the immigrants did not understand a word of English the captain said. Is your sea-sickness any better?"

"Yes, but the conditions make me want to vomit. What more can happen? It is bewildering. How terrible for the families. Not even their own religious priest to officiate." Said Teresa.

"Do not think about this mess. Tell me, what are your favorite things. What do you like?" They were busily chatting away on personal things, when Teresa said, "Monty, look. The woman behind you, near the center. She is in labor." The rocking motion of the ship had caused premature labor. The woman groaned in pain. An old, humped man pushed his way through the throng around her. His hands were crippled from arthritis and he hobbled from a limp. "Let me through. I am a doctor." Said the humble, struggling man.

It was not long before the doctor handed the fetus to her husband standing nearby. He carried the still-born to the rail's side and mercifully laid it to rest in the waves' rhythmic motion of the sea's womb. Passengers in different tongues prayed a plaintive funeral chorus. The doctor tried to comfort the woman in her distraught despair. The immigrants' wailful prayers echoed their doubts and fears of ever reaching a full-term passage or new life ahead.

Teresa was visibly shaken over the pitiful mother. Monty tried to get her mind on something else, and decided to tell the story of a cousin crossing the raging sea on the Francis and Elizabeth, and how France floundered in a sea of economic disaster. He began, "The people were starving and screaming for economic relief."

"Monty, that is not the way to start your story."

"What do you mean."

"Have you forgotten what I asked of you?"

"Oh, you mean . . ., I forgot.

Simon says . . .

The desparate king called for the clever, Swiss financier, Jacques Necker. However, monarcial law denied Necker naturalization because he was a Protestant. Only French citizens could serve on the King's Council. The king solved the dilemma by creating the new department of Directory of the Royal Treasury, and appointed Necker, Director-General of Finance. This action stirred a glimmer of weak, but hopeful change for the people who called and considered, Necker a genius.

Darkness came early during the beginning weeks of 1777. The family gathered around the fire in their four rockers. "It is sure a rainy, muddy month. The winds should be drying the mud by now."

"Do not worry mom. We will get the room built before seedtime." Said Joe.

"I remember the mud-ball you made for my birthday." She proceeded to relate her story to Rita.

"Oh, no. Not the baby story, mom. I am twenty-one years old and. . . ."

"And will always be my baby, son."

Pete grinned at Joe's annoyance and asked Andy, "Dad, did you know there are Frenchmen and others from the continent still joining the American colonies in the war against England, and making names for themselves through their distinquished services?"

"Pete, do you remember when a youth, I spoke to you about Baron von Frederick Steuben."

"Yes, he is the Prussian who served in King Frederick II's army and was made Major General and appointed Inspector-General of George Washington's army."

"Yes, I heard from Otto Schmiller one of his sons, the one who is a sailor, wrote home Baron von Fredrick Steuben had written an army manual for the United States, and the baron was so content in America, he planned to stay."

"Lafayette is over there, too. Read where the practical, common sense Rousseauian, Albert Gallatin, sailed to America, too; because he refused to command mercenary troops being raised to fight the colonists."

"Joe, is he English?" Asked Rita.

"No, he was born in Geneva, Switzerland."

"The war across the sea, how long has it been going on?" Asked Rita. Pete thought for awhile. "Colonies have been fighting about three years. Holland has joined us and the colonies against England."

"Thank heavons, it is across the sea." Lamented Elisa. Joe laid his book down, "I heard from the blacksmith, we had our first naval battle with the British just off our coast."

"That is getting too close."

"Lisa, do not worry. The seas may rage, but the land fighting is in America." Pete picked up his Rambler and began reading. "Here is an article about Europe's leading military men who have left for America. The latest is the Frenchman, Michel Ney."

"There have been so many, I lost count. Why do they cross the sea to fight for liberty when it is needed here?" Asked Elisa. Pete crushed the paper in his lap and snorted. "To enhance their military career. If it were really due to their belief, a cause for liberty, our monarchy would stamp them with treason. There are other reasons our leading military men volunteer. One key role is to mold the untrained American troops. There is also adventure. Count Benjamin Rumford was caught spying for the British, but he managed to flee back to England before getting caught."

"Read all you want about the sea and adventure. Just do not go sailing or seeking it." Said Elisa. Joe and dad exchanged knowing glaces. "Mom, there is so much going on over there. A David Bushnell invented a ship that travels under water, called a submarine."

"Son, it is impossible."

"No, mom. It has been done. He called it the Turtle."

"Benjamin Franklin is in France, and trying to get aid. The stupid clothes-horse, King Louis XVI, why can't he spend money on his own citizens?" Asked Rita. Everyone burst into laughter. "What I said is not funny, I mean it." Her statement created more laughter. Feeling left out, Rita got up and walked away. "Come back, Rita. We are laughing because you sound like great-grandpere. He never had a good word for the monarchy." Said Pete. "Oh." Rita shyly returned to her rocker. Elisa slid her rocker back from the fireplace and walked to the candle snuffer hanging from a rafter peg, "We all need our rest."

During the year, melancholy, famine, and strife shadowed their lives. France was grieving over the death of Jean Jacques Rousseau, who was buried in the Pantheon. Many mourned the loss of their philosopher and writer. It was his romantic outlook which offset the atheism of Voltaire and the rationalists, who had joined the Encyclopedists and produced Du contrat social.

From across the sea, most of the news during the lean and disparaging year was spread by sailors in French seaports via the grapevine and was mainly events of the American Revolution. Since the last French Indian War, where England ousted French interests in the new world, the French people were extremely concerned about the war of independence and were in favor of the colonists. The American cause for liberty captured French spirits, and held many spellbound in their own dreamy, far away hopes for liberty.

Pete put aside his paper, fuming, "The French Court better be more concerned with Paris conditions than wondering what color of roses Pierre Redoute is going to paint in their courts."

"Dad, I see what you have been complaining about through the years. Our monarcy has about decayed itself into nonexistence, and the violence seems to have no end."

"Joe, someday, mob rule will reign and heaven help us in its aftermath." Muttered Pete.

"I am afraid the captain across the sea, John Paul Jones, foretold the spirit of France, when he said, 'I have not yet begun to fight.'"

"Who is he?" Elisa asked.

"An American who fought a bloody battle off England's seacoast against Britain's more powerful ship, Serapis. His flagship, Bonhomme Richard, had only forty-two guns."

"The Dutch are in their fourth war." Said Joe.

"How depressing. Can't you men discuss other news? The queen gave birth to Marie Therese, the Madame Royal." Said Elisa.

"Oh, that is news. What is the word on the baby and queen?" Rita asked.

"It was of little interest to the people I met in the village." Said Andy.

"You mean they were not talking about it?"

"Not a word. The talk in the tavern was rebellious. Job Matlin brought in a paper from his bookstore. One of Marat's, L'Ami du peuple, listed the food servings at a recent royal ball. There was not a soul in the tavern, who did not feverishly participate in the verbal uproar. I shut-up and watched, stunned to see how the one word--food, had solidified all into one emotion of hate."

Elisa looked at Pete and humorously asked, "What food was that, kraut and neckbones?"

"While most of France starves, they dined on a banquet of soup, turkey, goose, ham, beef, pickled pork legs, breads, pheasant eggs, curries, puddings, jellies, wines and beer."

"That was one meal?" Joe questioned.

"One meal. It was is a banquet, a serving of several foods at one setting." Pete answered.

"Andy, how did the uproar end?" Rita asked.

"It simmered down into laughter when Bartholomew Vervins, the baker, said his youngest son was a boulanger in a Paris bakery and made deliveries to the royal balls. Bartholomew said the latest gossip among the bakers came during a delivery, where one witnessed the snobbery of a royal quadrille. It was hilarious the way he mimicked gestures and steps, as he told how each lady was led out to dance in the order of her social position." Andy smirked and added, "Unequivocally a parade of unequality."

Joe was twenty when Rita gave birth in 1780, to the new family member, Lambert Lucas de Regnier. The room addition had been completed and the seed-drill was making quick work of field labors. Pete left, to spread the news in the village and surrounding neighbors. Luke was born and all went according to Hoyle."

Pete had stopped at the tavern and before he sat, Francois Bonet rose from a table, waving, "Pete, a letter came for you. It is at my livery. A currior from the Alsace-Lorraine area brought it."

In the past, members of the Regnier clan had been divided in their allegiances, due to the ambiguity of their fatherland, Alsace Lorraine. Pete's branch was known as the French branch and retained the original pronunciation of their name Ra-nya, while brothers of Peter Antoine I, had looked upon themselves more German in customs and changed their pronunciation and spelling to Reg-ner.

Pete returned and scurred into the house, when Elisa asked, "Did you tell Ursala Voiter our good news?"

"No, did not stop at the seamstress. She will get the news. It spreads fast in the village." He pulled the letter from his pocket and waved it in front of Elisa.

"Who is it from?" Andy asked, before Elisa had opened her mouth to speak.

"Cousin Mathias. They are going to America and asked if we want to go with them. He writes since conditions are worsening, he thought we would be interested. Asked us to think about it. I know Lisa and I would not considered it. Joe, you and Rita might give it some thought."

Elisa scowled at Pete and asked, "Oh no, Pete. How can you say that?"

"Rita what do you think about it?"

"I would not want to leave mom and dad. What do you think, Joe?"

"The idea is appealing, but no. I would rather stay."

"I am trying to remember when I last saw Mathias. Guess, he was about twelve. It has been too dangerous for families to travel, we might as well be oceans apart." Moaned Andy.

Pete gazed at the letter as he explained its contents. "He says three of their families are going. His two brothers and his own. They leave July 30 on the Francis and Elizabeth, down the Rhine to Rotterdam and upon docking at America, plan to enter Canada."

"What? Wonder why he does not stay in America? Canadian provincial regulations there require, upon entering, that one must take an oath of alligiance to the King of Great Britain. That is true, because I read it in a book at Job's store." Joe added.

"Well, Mathias does not say. Did write he plans to pay 66 shillings for some land and sign the mortgage. I would guess he has had correspondence with a Canadian."

Elisa asked, "I wonder how long the trip takes."

Pete pointed to the second page of the letter, and read. "We have been informed the voyage will take about seven to twelve weeks."

Rita gasped, uttering, "That is awful. I hope he knows what he is doing."

"It is a treacherous voyage but crossing the Atlantic in July should be the safest time of the year." Said Joe.

"The seven seas," Pete shoke his head, "are always unpredictable and risky. Besides, I have heard bad reports on how immigrants are charged exhorbant fees and packed like eggs in a crock into the bottom of a ship's filthy quarters where many die from the conditions before reaching America. I will write him tonight, so he will be sure to receive my answer before leaving. Think I will forewarn him of the reports being told about many of the voyage's bad conditions, and how word has gotten back to France from immigrants who survived and wrote home about the voyage."

"Be sure to ask him to write, and let us know he arrived safely." Said Elisa.

"I have finished sinking the post-rails in the woods. We can begin transhumance any day." Said Joe.

"I have been trying to figure out what order we should move the livestock. You say you have railed three areas?" Pete asked.

"Yes. A central one and one on each side."

"If we rope all the litters to their mother, we can lead the whole bunch to an area and save alot of trips." Said Andy.

"That is what we will do. Do the pigs go first?" Asked Joe.

"No, they have become so lean during the winter, I want to try and fatten the swine. Better take ol' Ox, before we need him for plowing. Then the cow, sheep and the goat last." Answered Pete.

"Joe, have you any of those post rails left?" Asked Elisa.

"Yes, I have stacked them by the rock pile."

"Pete, would you make a crib-pen for Luke? Like the one your dad made for Joe when he was small?"

Pete thought for a moment. "I guess Luke will be crawling by the time you women work the garden. I will see to it."

Across the sea in America and in France, people had cause to bless and hail the many French heros. Marquis de Lafayette was ordered by General George Washington to block Cornwallis. Admiral de Grass succeeded in repulsing the British ships that occupied Cheaspeake Bay. Generals Lafayette and Rochambeau made the final and decisive action of the American Revolution by moving their troops south to Virginia and battled the British troops entrenched in Yorktown, where General Cornwallis surrendered on October 19, 1781.

Pete and Joe returned from the village after mailing their letter to Mathias. Immediately upon their entering, Elisa asked, "Did you find Luke's birthday toy?" Joe, playfully, pulled a book from a bundle and laid it on the table. "We both decided to give him this."

"What? A book? The British Prison Ship? You both are as crazy as King George. Show me, what you got Luke?"

"Found a jack-in-the-pulpit. Show her dad." Pete wound it up, placed the toy on the table and lifted the lid. Out jumped a clownish figure dressed in brilliant colored garb.

"It is perfect." Elisa squealed in delight.

"He will love it." Said Rita as she curiously poked at the book, opened it and asked, "What is this book about?"

"Ravages upon the high seas. Philip Freneau, a sea captain during the American Revolution, wrote about his experience on a British prison ship. Although people in Job's bookstore were praising and talking about it, I do not think you would enjoy reading it."

"Joe, what are you laughing about?"

"I was thinking, you women would be more interested in the villagers' talk about the escapades of Catherine Grand and her third lover."

"Oh, what were they saying? Tell us about it." Asked Rita.

Overseas the American Revolution continued and on the sea, England was being threatened from commanders as John Paul Jones and American privateers. However, England was more worried about an invasion from American allies, who had gained control of the English Channel--France, Spain, and the Dutch.

Luke's second birthday fell on the day the Great Seal of the United States was adopted. Luke was walking, talking and at times, quite vexing. The year was especially lean as the family had no spare animals to butcher. Another year of increased tailles, poor harvests, livestock too thin to breed, disease rampant, and increased arrests. With conditions continuing to worsen, the peasantry and villagers began to express revolutionary attitudes.

"Dad, remember the book I got last year, The British Prison Ship? This paper briefly states that the Great Seal of the United States was first being used on a document granting General Washington authority to initiate a prisoner exchange with the British. Does the paper have any more news about it? I would like to find out more about the prisoner exchange."

Pete replied, "I remember the book. No, the only item about America is one about Thomas Jefferson enacting a law where anyone can, with a legitimate will, upon his death, set free his slaves. A virtuous act all right, but I would say it is more of a final gasping, a grasp for atonement."

CHAPTER 13: THE BALLOON

"Monty your family has always been interested in America. Just think, you will be the first to get there."

"I plan to write them about the country and her customs." Then he became very saddened at the thought of being far from home. "God, I miss them, already."

"Of course. You have good memories to miss. Bad memories, you do not miss. Another story." She begged.

"We are upon the raging sea. How is your sea-sickness? Any better?"

"Yes. You say tomorrow my sickness should be over?"

"By the third day it is usually over. I am much better, today. Another story, eh? Well, let me wrestle with this a bit. Must remember to start it correctly.

Simon says . . .

Rita told Elisa, "I do not know if I want to take Luke out in this winter weather."

"Peez, peez, mommie. I wan-na see da bah-hoon." Begged Luke

"I suppose so."

Pete was eager for his family to see the balloon, but not eager to take them into Paris. Jacques Montgolfier and his brother had invented a hot-air balloon a few years earlier, and the family missed the lift-off. Now, a much larger ballon was to be lifted. The floating balloon was the talk everywhere and created enormous interest. Flying was a new realm.

"Rita, let us pack the basket for the trip. We will need enough food for early lunch and we will probably get hungry on our way home." Said Elisa.

Joe stood in the doorway with his hand propping it open, "Rita, come see what dad has done." Before anyone could catch him, Luke zoomed out of the door and into the cold outside. Joe dashed after him and dragged him into the house. He sat Luke in a chair, shoke a finger at him and scolded, "Listen here little fellow, never go outside without your coat and hat, or without asking. Now, you sit on the chair as punishment until I say you may get down."

Luke looked at Joe sheepishly, too stubborn to cry. He looked to see if Andy was near, but he was in the stable. He always understood and sympathized. Luke sat at attention and with spiteful intent to aggravate, wiggled his toes making his clogs bang against the stone floor. Elisa walked past, grabbed his shoulder and shoke it, "Stop it, this instant." She put on her coat and left with Joe. Joe wrapped an arm around Elisa as he led her towards the south side. "Rita, dad has had these staves soaking under the ice in the brook. He brought them in, warmed them and bent them over the cart."

"Why did he do that?"

"You will see."

"Joe, help me hoist these skins." Joe looked at the covering and helped pull it over the staves. "Looks as though you have stitched every hide we had."

"Yes, son, I have been saving and drying skins for over a year. My plan is now complete."

"Oh, look inside, Joe. Dad has lined it with woolpacks."

"To keep my family warm during our trip to Paris."

After Joe and Rita had gone back into the house, Pete slide his flintlock musket under the fleece. He had not made up his mind if the trip to Paris would be safe. He had heard rumors of uprisings. But there were rumors of a Paris filled with gaiety, wit, scandals, opera and brilliant, flamboyant clothing. Women in huge gowns with powdered wigs bedecked with jewels and ribbons. Men in silks, satins and velvets. This was the reality of Paris and the revolutionary rumors must be thoughts of dreamers. Yes, they would make a safe journey to Paris and see the balloon. The event of the year. But, Pete did not remove his musket.

Pete spotted the black kettle on the table. "See, the old pot is on. You women too busy to fix vittles for us men? What is all the hustling about?"

"Sit down and eat. We are getting the clothing laid out for tomorrow." Said Elisa. Pete looked at a the stack of small stockings, "You going put all those leggings on Luke?"

Luke awoke early and awakened everyone. At the table, he asked, "Go now?" Rita looked at Elisa, closed her eyes and shoke her head. "Young man, we eat our breakfast. Then grandpere yokes the ox. Then we bundle up and carry our things and pack them into the cart."

"Then Luke get in 'un ride?"

"Yes." Andy spread his arms as Luke dashed into them. Elisa

was the first to leave the house. Pete pulled the cart near the door and loaded it with a bale of hay and a small barrel of water. "Pete, when did you make the cover and double yoke?" Asked Elisa.

"The other day, when I decided the cow could also pull with the ox. A long trip, you know. Joe and I pulled the skins over the bent staves." She inspected the wheels. "These are wider wheels." Pete boosted her into the cart. "Lisa, the cart rides better with wider rims."

"Oh, look at this warm wool inside." She snuggled into the fleecy piles. Pete boosted Rita and Luke into the cart, "Hope you are not full of questions." Then Pete helped Andy get himself in and seated comfortably.

"Where are we going?" Asked Andy, as one of his spells began to confused him.

"To da' bah-hoon, gampa."

Pete climbed into the cart, seated himself on the plank and grasped both reins, "All right, Joe, you can let go of the animals." Joe left the ox and cow, and jumped into the cart. "Let's go." On December 1, 1783, the cart lumbered down the road and made a right turn north onto the Paris road. In the early morning, steam spouted from the animals nostrils. They had not gone far, when Rita shouted, "There goes dad and mom in their cart. Wish they had a covered cart." When the animals pulled the cart past the first bend, Pete spotted Jacque's cart trailing behind. "We are apt to see a lot of carts today. Could be a crowded road."

"Everyone wants to see the balloon." Said Joe.

Elisa shouted above the rumbling wheels, "We are snug and warm in here. You two are out in the cold." She pulled a couple sheepskins from the pile and wrapped one around each man. Luke had been busily going from side to side of the cart looking at the passing roadside. Soon he curled himself on Andy's lap. The young and old among the fleece, soon fell asleep.

They came upon a lengthy stretch of straight road and saw cart after cart, heading along the road to Paris. Pete sighed, "Wish the event was on the outskirts of Paris."

Rita asked, "Where is it?" Pete heaved another sigh and said, "At the Gardens of Tuileries." Rita pulled excitedly on Joe's shoulder. "You know, I have always wanted to see it and never have. Will we see royalty? Oh, what fun."

Pete thought of his great grandpere, his grandpere and his dad, whose age was dulling his senses with occasional spells. He recalled how each held monarchism in disgust, while others held monarchy in a zealous, religious veneration. He remembered his grandpere's remarks of disgust about Louis XIV's grandiose palace that took more than thirty years to build. Peasants all over France were subjected to royal taxes to pay the many architects, craftsmen and builders. Vivid recollections came to mind. His grandpere's frequent, sarcastic usage of the king's, "L'etat c'est moi " ("I am the state"), and arguments with friends and strangers who felt the king's reign was one of brilliance. His grandpere was not silent about the king's revocation of the Edict of Nantes that drove friends and valuable citizenry into exile; nor of the economic conditions left from the demands of wars. He and other peasants griped about the farm-rent to landlord's estates raised by agents, who gave a portion to the king's agent, and then pocketed the rest. Burden of payment fell upon the peasantry, including the lion's share of tithes for the Church, taxes and numerous royal perks.

Grandpere's family had distinquished themselves in literary and art circles, which allowed them to be tenant farmers, but did not lessen his concern for the majority, who had to pay by their daily labors or in goods and were not allowed to harvest their crops until the royal wagons took their share. When Louis XV became king, his grandpere, with the eye of a hawk, had grown up watching the weak, indecisive monarchy rotten from the influences of Mme. de Pompadour and Mme. Du Barry. A reign that cost France almost all her colonies and did nothing to ease internal conditions that worsened each year. Then Louis XVI became King of France; a fat, gluttonous, gentle ineffective king, who bent in any direction the wind blew. Times had not changed.

What would his grandpere say about the fripperies of Paris aristocracy? Pete knew his grandpere's viewpoints never leaned toward revolutionary ideas. Public opinion now had the ring of his grandpere's convictions, but with the added and fearful tone of revolt.

Would grandpere have taken his family on a trip of possible danger to witness an invented balloon? Pete wondered, as he slide both reins into one hand and his other hand reached down, to feel under the fleece and assure himself the musket was there. Elisa and Rita huddled in the wooly sheepskins playing word games and giggling.

"Dad, you are awfully quiet. Thinking about Paris rumors?" Asked Joe.

"Somewhat. The unexpected can catch one unprepared."

"I heard Paris is agog over this event and people have already arrived from all parts of the continent for the first performance of The Marriage of Figaro by Beaumarchais. Said Joe.

"Tis no wonder, son. The king's banning of it the past three years only created more interest."

"Why was it banned?"

"I heard it was a political and social satire, a play that gave rise to thought and whispers of conspiracy."

Won't the masses be too caught up in this rivelry to stir up trouble?" Asked Joe.

"You speak only about those who can afford to go to the opera. Let us hope that will be the case. My question is, how will fat aristocracy mix with starved peasantry?"

They rumbled down the road, and Pete began watching both sides of the road. The road to Paris cut through heavily wooded terrain. He leaned over to whisper in Joe's ear, "I read in Le Journal General de France, there was an increase in travelers' assaults and robberies by roving bands of ruffians. There is a price on their heads, but the woods hides them well. If I quickly hand you the reins, that is your signal to takeover. I will be reaching for my musket hidden beside me."

"I will be ready. I can see into the woods, but of course those hedges and undergrowth could hide men, if they were crawling."

"This area is not bad. Ahead is the last bend. Afterwards there is a stretch where the road dips down and runs through a ravine. High embankments on either side could allow an easy jump into our cart."

Joe slowly nodded his head, "I will watch the right side and you the left." Pete leaned towards Joe, and said, "Do not want to alarm the women, but we must make sure we leave in time so as not to be driving through this stretch after sunset." The road extended into a clearing as they neared Paris. "Dad, why are all those carts jammed behind one another?"

"The carts probably had to slow down, due to the street crowds up ahead." Soon they were near Jacque's cart and he turned and waved. Joe pointed, "Look, I see Rita's family up there."

"Joe, here is what I want you to do when we get behind them. Go to Jacque's cart and tell him we will park together and leave together in a caravan. Then run up to Mike's cart and tell him the same."

It was still morning when they reached the crowded cobblestone streets of Paris with vehicles and pedestrians trying to race forward, but held at a slow pace from the congestion. Vendors sold wares from pull-carts and hollered at the passing stream of people, those in velvet curtained carriages and those in wagons and carts. Throngs agilely dodged past the many maimed and blind beggars leaning against the buildings. Some ladies were in simple, long dresses with capelets. There were men with staves, in bloomers gathered at the knee above their long stockings. There were women in skirts and blouses covered with shawls, aprons and bonnets, who pulled weary children along on foot.

Rita did not want to miss anything, she stared at everything. "Mom, look at the stores, how big and high. See the gentlemen swaggering down this old dirty street. Ain't he spiffy in his silks, satins and velvet? Guess, he is carrying his hat so he will not mess his wig. Over there. See the lady? All those jewels and ribbons in her wig. How utterly beautiful. Oh, I see a soldier. Look at his plumed helmet, and the gorgeous horse."

Such were the sights that engrossed Rita's youthful curiosity. Elisa was not impressed. She watched a bedecked courtesan trying to enter her carriage with a gown so enormous she could barely enter. Pete was noticing the air of contempt shown from the aristocracy towards the peasantry as gentlemen sniffed from gilded snuffboxes and arrogantly whisked lace kerchiefs in the peasant faces. Wealthy women peaked from their lowered eyelids in disdain at the wretched, starving people.

Elisa sat silent, in despair. Never had she seen so many gaunt-eyed, toothless, boney people with open festering sores, shuffling along in shredded, patched rags and feet wrapped in rags held on with tied string at the ankles. Some carried belongings in ragged sacks tossed over a shoulder. The majority of wretched beings traveled down one side of the street, while the opposite side of the street was lined with wealthy carriages, carts and an occasional horseman. Elisa noticed the crowd's excitement was a frantic frenzy, rather than anticipation. The chatter was filled with screeching tones. Everyone headed to the Gardens of the Tuileries.

Mike Gautier pulled his cart to one side. The Gardens had filled with crowds of about two hundred thousand watchers standing and sitting. Jacque pulled his cart next to Mike's and Pete followed.

Pete saw the crowd push forward, forcing the gates and railings down and gasped, "That was close." Joe stepped off the cart to water the cow and ox.

"Wann-tout." Said Luke.

Pete told Rita, "We will all stay in this cart. Crowd could get unruly."

Everyone was talking and the roar of the conversation suddenly stopped. The balloonists had appeared. The crowd roared cheers until the men stepped into the basket. Then all became quiet. Up, up the balloon went. Luke had both hands in the air, as if to catch the balloon. He jumped up and down, yelling, "pretty, pretty," as he clapped his hands. Andy stared, his mouth agap, it was beyond his comprehension. "What is it?" He implored.

"Gampa, da' bah-hoon." Said Luke, jumping up and down.

People in the crowd prayed, fainted, and gawked in messmerized amazement. When the balloon sailed over the crowd the balonists swung their flags in salute. Pete hollered, "Mike. Let us go, before the crowd moves." Pete goaded the animals and they headed away.

"Why are we leaving?" Asked Andy.

"We go home, gampa. Go home."

Jacque and Mike followed closely behind. Swarms of people ran past them. The mobs moved faster than the carts and scattered across the street. It was not the orderly street procession as before. Each cart was amidst crowds of raucous revelers, still chanting and ranting about the marvels of the event.

Luke tugged on Rita's arm, "I am hungry." Rita opened the basket and broke off a piece of bread to pacify him. "Grandpere said we will eat after we pass the first bend in the road.

"How far? How long?" Asked Luke.

"Eat your bread, Luke."

"This crowd should lessen, once we have reached the outskirts of the city." Said Pete.

Rita screamed and grabbed Luke's leg as he was being pulled across the edge of the cart. The straggly, bushy-haired woman stopped pulling on Luke, once she took the bread from Luke's hand. Luke cried in horror as Rita tried to sooth his fears. Joe had turned around, but not in time to grab Luke. Pete was unable to goad the animals any faster in the crowd. "Rita, best you keep Luke in your lap until we get into the woods." Elisa reached for Luke, "Here, let me hold the poor child." She hugged him and began singing a folk song.

Jacque stopped his cart when he heard Luke's scream. "Go on. Go," hollered Pete, and the caravan moved forward, but only at the pace of the mob. As they approached each intersecting city street, several people would depart from the throng. There were only a few streets left to cross. Pete and Joe glanced at each other and sighed knowingly. At that moment, each felt the poke of a stave cut into their skin and slid up their backs. Rowdy, malicious men had hooked the fleecy skins drapped over Pete and Joe's shoulders and ran with the fleece flopping atop each staff and their staves held in mid-air A group ran after the men, clawing and yanking at the fleece, trying to take the sheepskins.

"Stay calm, Joe." Said Pete. Rita scurried to the back of the cart, "I will get you another skin before you freeze."

"No. Wait until we get to the woods. Push all those skins down in the cart, so they can not be seen. Cover them with the sacking and scatter the straw." Pete angrily said, "Damnit. This mob could easily push our cart over in a mad rush to steal our fleece. They are cold, shivering in tattered rags and half-crazed from hunger."

The winter sun was beginning to set as Jacque's cart pulled into his farm road. Further ahead were the Gautiers. Pete waved as Mike continued north. Pete goaded the animals into their roadway towards home. The trip had ended without severe mishap. Pete pulled up to the doorway. "Dad, you help the women and grandpere. I will take care of the animals and cart."

Elisa alit from the cart with a sigh, "We will not be having pots a l'avoine, but we sure are not starving." Rita followed, carrying Luke. "Oh, he is asleep. He has had an emotional day. He can rest until we get supper ready. As rambuntious as he is, it is odd to see him worn-out." Pete gave his grandson an adoring glance, "We are all spent." Then he settled in his rocker, shuffling nearby papers. "I have not read the Affiches de Paris, yet. See if there is more information on immigration? It is the main topic of conversation in the tavern and coffee houses."

Rita returned from putting Luke into bed and walked over to Pete, affectionately rubbing his shoulder. "Dad, you planning to go to America?" She leaned over his shoulder to read his paper, "Oh, it says the Empress of China set sail from New York. Coming here, perhaps, for you?"

Pete turned and pinched Rita's cheek as he replied, "With conditions they way they are in Europe, imagine vessels will be carrying hundreds of our countrymen across the sea. But not me."

"Not me? What are you discussing?" Joe asked, as he slammed the door, stomped his feet and bent down to remove his boots. In stocking feet he sped to the fireplace for warmth, and then flopped into his rocker.

Andy limped over to the fire. "I think I am having one of my spells."

Elisa looked at Andy. "Dad, you go rest. I will wake you for supper." She turned him around and guided him to his room.

"Your dad says he is not going to America." Said Rita, grinning coyly.

"No, do not reckon he will join us." Said Joe as he sneaked a glance at his dad. Pete dropped the paper in his lap and stared at Joe, "You, two, still thinking about going to America?" Rita and Joe burst into laughter. Pete said no more, he picked up his paper and intently read, ignoring their clowning.

Screams came from the bedroom. Rita rushed to Luke. She picked him up and walked into the room, as Andy came limping into the room and asked, "Is Luke hurt?"

"No. Luke, sit yourself at the table. He had a bad dream. We know what it was about." Pete went over and placed the black pot of soup on the table and handed Luke a piece of bread. "It is over now. What did you think of the balloon?" Luke wildly chewed his bread and clapped his hands.

"I wish, what we saw was only a bad dream." Said Elisa.

CHAPTER 14: OLD AND NEW SECRETS

"Monty, your story jogged my memory. I can remember my parents recalling stories about the balloon and how it turned all Paris into a mad-house. Everyone racing to see the balloon."

"See, your family had their stories."

"Suppose so, but can not remember them."

"It takes alot of re-telling stories before one remembers. There is the captain with our lunch ration. The roll is beginning to taste pretty good, now that I feel better."

"I have an appetite today." Said Teresa.

"What do you know, we have black bread instead of the roll. Things are looking up."

They said little as they indulged in the welcome repast. It was another nice, brisk day and the sunlight on the waves created forms in Monty's imagination of water shafts like buildings and the sparkle of windows in a far away city. Then he saw them, "Look at the porpoises. I guess, that is what they are. Do you know?"

"No, but how nice to see? I think it is time for another story."

"You are not tired of my stories?"

"No. They make this horried trip bearable."

"All right. It begins when the family had little time to wonder about the future of France, or about Holland still in its fourth war. Seedtime was near. Dire needs forced them to create a more frugal saving plan."

"Monty, you are forgetting again." Said Teresa.

"Oh, Simon says . . .,

Luke watched the men planting and noticed the seed-drill spilt grain as it turned each corner row. He carefully picked up each seed and stuffed it into his pockets. His baby fat waddled as he walked to the house and through the opened door. He proudly dumped the seeds from his pockets onto the table.

"Mommie. Gamma, see. Seeds."

"Merci. Your dad will be proud." Said Elisa. Rita wrapped an arm around Luke, "Where did you find this treasure?" Luke gazed into his mother's eyes, "Do-un my feeled shore. Throwed rocks at birds that eat seeds daddy plants. Saw seeds fall." Rita went over to the wall, took a small pail from a peg and handed it to Luke. "Son, you have yourself a man's job." Luke's face beamed as she spoke, "Luke have two jobs. Luke hit birds. Luke get seeds."

Rita rested her hand on Elisa's shoulder, "It is nice how Luke's rambunctiousness has turned into a constructive path?" Elisa laughed in response, "It isn't from his dad. He was a wild, active one until age nine. Must get it from his great grandpere." She had caught Rita's attention. "He was a remarkable man, wasn't he? Tell me about him."

"Pete has not left much to tell. I have listened while Pete passed stories on to Joe and again to Luke. And mom, bless her soul. How I miss her. Tears moistened her eyes, she was . . . "

"Mom, should I pound some grain? Is this enough flour for today's bread?" Asked Rita. She waited awhile, then asked, "Mom, soon woodland flowers will bloom. Let us pick bouquets and walk down our path and visit the church cemetery." Elisa embraced Rita and clung to her, "That will be a comfort to us both, my child."

Pete was the first to arrive for dinner. He propped his hoe against the wall and sat himself at the table. "Glad tomorrow's Sunday. Been a long, hot week. Covering seeds behind the seed-drill keeps one hustling. Sowing by hand, gave a man time to plug along. Joe led the ox at a fast pace, figuring we could finish today. Luke did a good job scaring the birds away. Got tickled at his squatting routine. He would stand at the end of a row facing my back and fling rocks at birds. Between his bird attacks he would be bobbing up and down. Was not until I got to the end of the row, that I figured out what he was doing. He was gathering seeds the drill spilled and dropping them into his pail."

"You men hungry?" Asked Rita as Joe and Luke entered. Luke sat the pail down and dashed into her arms. "We done, mommie."

"Luke has almost a full pail. I tried to carry the pail, but he refused to let go. We had finished planting, but he would not leave until he had done every row. We men pitched in and finished. Didn't we son?"

"Nuf seed for Ox."

"Luke, you got some there for the hens?" Andy chuckled and hobbled up the stable steps from feeding the hens.

"Rita, sure is good bread." Said Joe, as he chomped on a hunk. Andy put his bread down and waited until his laughter ceased. Luke mimicked Andy and began giggling. Elisa took offense, "What are you laughing about? Rita made this bread and it is fresh and delicious." Andy said, "Just remembering." Again he began chuckling. "Well, I never. You owe Rita an explanation."

"I was thinking about the time Joe told Pete, he met Rita in the bakery and Pete asked if it meant she could not bake bread."

"My seeds make bread." Luke blurted. Pete reached down to shake Luke's hand. "That is right, Luke. We men worked hard today. We need our rest. About bedtime, eh?"

"Bedtime. Men get tired, don't we daddy?"

Luke never awakened too eagerly, or cheerfully on Sundays. It was the day he had to sit in a pew longer than he cared to. "No clogs. No, no." Said Luke. Rita tapped him on the butt, "You will not go to church barefooted." Luke munched his lips together, curled the botton lip into a pouty flap, and spouted, "Pierre does."

"Do not argue, Luke. The poor child has no shoes. Be sure you say prayers of thanks that you do."

Joe came from the stable. "Livestock is fed. Everyone ready? Let's go."

In good weather the walk to the church was the short-cut along the path through the woods. It was a walk, paced by Andy's ability and gait. In bad weather, the cart traveled the lengthy southeast road. Elisa and Rita held one of Luke's hands as they walked to keep him from rummaging in the underbrush and soiling his clothes.

"Hear da bells." Luke uttered in sing-song fashion over and over, and skipped along. The church quickly filled. After community announcements the priest solomenly said, "The evils of Paris are not confined to the city. I am saddened to report that last Sunday, while coming to church, the Edward Conette family was assaulted. Their tithe stolen. They were in their cart traveling down the ravine road to the church and were accousted by robbers hiding in the woods. Regretfully, I must warn you each, to be cautious on your way coming and going to church. The faithful, and your tithes have become a target.

After church the congregation gathered in social tete-a-tete. Men discussed farming problems, politics, and the increasing famine. Women discussed fears of plague, famine and uprisings, then drifted into jovial tidbits of gossip.

"Have you heard?"

"No. What?"

"The queen's sinful ways? Not one paramour, but three." Voices gasped, asking, "Who?" Women counted the names off on their fingers. Some tittering, while others scorned.

"Lord Adhemar, Duke de Coigny and General Besenval."

There was enthusiastic talk about men who visited and returned to extoll liberty and tales of the government of independence in the new world of America. Words that enhanced dreams from the weary, struggling listeners.

Luke's cleanliness was not an issue walking home from church. He anxiously awaited this freedom. A time when he could inspect every rock, plant, and bug that came into view. Luke would dash ahead, scoot into underbrush bordering the path to satisfy his curiosity with nature's numerous surprises. Luke had forgotten about the tunnel, and in his excitement his imagination soared. Suddenly, he ran back to the group, hollering, "Hole. Pie-rup cave, like gampa read me. A hole."

"My word, he has found the tunnel." Muttered Pete, "If he can find it, we best think of a better way of hiding it."

"That is a job I can do tomorrow." Andy answered. As the family came closer Luke shouted, "See? See da' hole?" He scampered into it. Joe grabbed his feet and yanked him out. "That is not a pirate cave and not to be played in. I will tell you a story about it someday."

"Good story?"

Joe smiled, nodding his head. "Yes, the best story ever."

"When, daddy? When you tell best story ever?" Joe looked down at the little hand he held as they walked along, swinging it back and forth. "Son, it is a secret story. I will tell you at a secret time. You must wait till then." Luke's head jerked back, his eyes opened in awe, staring at Joe.

"Morning sunlight, how splendid," Rita thrust her head further out the window to hear the music of birds, rustling tree leaves, clucking hens, and an occasional cricket. She felt jubilant, yet fearful. Would she carry her child? Could she again endure a painful loss? She had kept her suspicious secret. The smell of breakfast nauseated her. She would need to tell, however, sharing her fear could be comforting.

Elisa noticed Rita had not awakened in time to help with breakfast. As Rita came from the bedroom, Elisa asked, "Are you feeling all right, dear?"

"Yes, what a beautiful morning." She smiled and joined the others gathered at the table. Rita sipped her tea.

"You are not eating anything." Elisa commented.

"My baby does not want anything."

"What? Really? Stammered Elisa. Joe stared at Rita, his jaw

slowly dropped lower and lower. "I thought you couldn't . . ."

Andy slapped the table as he said. "Beautiful day." Then, Luke slapped the table, saying, "Bootful day."

"Rita, I will milk the cow from now on. You can not be carrying a full milk bucket." Said Joe.

"That is no problem, yet."

"Young'un, best you obey your husband." Added Pete as Joe chimed in, "The cow has been moved to the farthest railed area in the woods."

"Mom, that is why I have been clumsy of late. The other day, dipping candles, I spilled tallow on my hand."

"Did you put suet on it?" Elisa asked anxiously.

"Yes, mom. At first, I shoke my hand in pain and the wax cooled and coated my fingers. I squeezed my hurt fingers, and as I rubbed on it, the wax slid off in a tube sacking. The tallow made a mold the size of my finger. It gave me an idea."

"What is it?" Asked Joe.

"Cheese. Mom, you take pride in making your cheese. . . ."

"I want cheese." Luke said, tugging at Rita's dress. Elisa turned to Joe, "Please, slice him a wedge from the wheel. I am listening to Rita. What were you saying?"

"We weave cloths for wrapping your cheese. We lose alot from heavy mold, so you make only a few at a time. Why not try dipping the wrapped cheese wheels into hot tallow? It should keep better."

Pete jumped up, almost upsetting the table and scaring Luke into tears. "Magnificent plan. Probably be able to make cheese from all our spare milk."

"And store it." Andy added.

"Yes. Store it." Joe repeated. Livestock would no longer get the spare milk. The milk would be destined for Elisa's waxy coated cheese. Rita gave them a birth to await, and the birth of an idea to develop Elisa could not wait. The next day she was at her churning.

"How many does that make, mom?" Asked Rita.

"Lost count." Laughed Elisa, beaming with pride over her latest cheese accomplishment. "May not be one of Italy's fancy Parmigiano-Reggianos, but it is mighty moist and tasty."

"Are you finished with this batch?"

"No, not until we date each wheel. Each must age twelve months. I inspect them, and if all right, they need to age for another six months."

Rita said, "I have tagged them. Ready for storage." Elisa proudly gathered her apron to make a carrying sack, and filled it with her treasured jewels. Rita rushed over to the steps, "I will get it mom," and yanked the pull-rope opening the root cellar. Elisa carefully hung each wheel from the special bar Pete installed.

"Mom, today is another splendid day. Let us walk to the cemetery. Flowers are in bloom."

"Yes, and on the return trip, stop in the woods for a picnic of cheese and crackers. You stay here, child. I will get Luke from the field. We will see which Luke prefers, weeding with the men or a picnic."

"Pick-neek? Eat in da' woods? Don't wait for supper?"

"Right, Luke. I will put goodies in the basket and we will be off, as soon as I get another basket for our flowers." Said Rita.

"Fowers? Pick fowers at pick-neek?"

"Yes. We need your help to gather flowers to fill the basket."

"I find pity ones. Jus' pity ones, momma."

"I forgot, Rita. Pete said to take the dogs when we go into the woods. If we do not, he will notice, and angrily leave fieldwork to stop us. You know how he can worry."

"Luke, you come back here. Stay with us." Shouted Elisa as Luke and the dogs raced ahead. Luke ran stumbling over rocks and sticks with clenched fistfuls of flower-heads to drop blossoms into the basket and run off for more.

"He loves this flower-hunt. I suppose, I should show him how to pick a flower, so as not to pull its blossom off."

"Never you mind. He is doing a fine job. These flowers are to show love, not for show."

Rita took Luke's hand and followed Elisa to a familiar marker. "What dat say?" Asked Luke as he pointed to the carved printing on the stone. "That says, Peter Antoine de Regnier. He was your great, great, great grandpere. Over here is your great, great, grandpere, Daniel."

"Gaiter than gait-gampa, Andy?"

"No. Older than grandpere. Now you spread some flowers over the graves. We put flowers here to show we still love and remember."

"Gamma's putting fowers ober dar. What dat stone say?"

"Let us go see." Rita knelt by the stone and read the name, "Maria Louisa de Regnier. She was your great grandmere." Luke gave her a puzzled look; reached into the basket and dropped his fistful of crushed flowers. "Older dan gamma?"

"Right, son. You are so smart." Said Rita. Luke looked towards

Elisa, wanting her to share in the praise. "Why gamma kneel ober dare? She no haf fowers." Without waiting for an answer, Luke grabbed flowers from the basket with both hands and ran to Elisa to offer her the bunch. She silently reached out and took them. Luke dashed back to Rita in tears. "Gamma's crying. Why gamma cry?" Rita wrapped Luke in her arms, "Because she misses him. It hurts to miss someone. Remember when your daddy went to work at the tobacco shop?"

"Go wok."

"Yes. He was gone all day and you cried. You missed him." Luke nodded his head sadly as he remembered. "Gamma sad."

"Now we go to the stone over there. It says Arthur William de Regnier."

"Who dat?" Asked Luke. Rita knelt by the grave, pulled Luke closely into her lap, "Artie was my baby. Your brother. I miss him very much." Luke looked at Rita and patted her cheek. "Sad mommie. Miss Artie. Put fowers here." Luke's fists flew back and forth tossing flower heaps upon the small grave.

Elisa walked over to Rita and asked, "Is Luke ready to picnic?" He jumped from Rita's lap, shouting, "Da' woods. Da' woods." Walking back along the path, Rita said, "Mom, there is a secret spot. One that means alot to Joe and I. Let us picnic there."

"All right." Elisa watched silently, wondering if Rita's spot was the same secret place she and Pete held dear. It was not too far down the pathway. Elisa watched, as Rita set the basket down between two extending roots under the same hickory tree. Must tell Pete, Elisa thought, as she remembered their polonaise of long ago.

They walked from the woods towards home, when one dog came out of a thicket carrying a hare it had killed. Elisa patted and praised Spookie. "We have our supper." She took a cloth from the picnic basket and wrapped the hare before putting it in the basket. Luke ran ahead with the dogs and playfully chased them in circles.

"It has been a lovely day. Luke sure likes your cheese, Mom. He probably will not eat much supper."

"Yes, he is liable to fall asleep before supper from the way he has been racing the dogs."

"Look. See Joe over there? He is leading the swine to the railed woodland. Bet he brings the cow back."

"Rita, you will still not do the milking, child. Tummy is getting too big." Joe saw them and waved. Luke noticed, and took off on a run across the clearing towards Joe.

"Let him go, Rita. He needs to run off some of the energy."

Elisa and Rita entered the house and heard a strange, loud racket. "Merci. What is that?" Elisa set the basket down and hurried to the stable. "Pete, what are you doing?"

"You nosey woman. Hoped to get this done before you returned."

"Finish what?"

"Grinding this stone, it is almost the right size."

"Right size for what?"

"To throw at nosey women. This is man's art. A secret." Andy, sitting nearby, noticed Elisa's displeasure and added, "It is a tool." Exasperated, Elisa went to the cooking area and joined Rita.

"The old goat is grinding a rock, Rita. For what, he would not say. Sat there smuggly telling me it was man's art--a secret."

"Men can sure be arrogant at times."

"Andy said some kind of tool. I suppose Pete will keep up the noise until supper. Let us hurry and get the rabbit on the table."

When the noise stopped, Elisa heard Pete talking to Joe, who was trying to get Bossie to go through the south door of the stable. "Guess old Bossie, prefers the woodland." When Bossie finally trotted into the stall, Joe asked. "You have more grinding to do on that stone?"

"Just about have it," Joe.

"How are you coming on yours?"

"Not much more."

Elisa set the platter of rabbit on the table with a thud. "Listen to those men. What can they possibly be talking about?" Rita poured buttermilk into the cups. "Up to something. I know that much." No sooner had Joe entered the room, then Elisa said, "Supper's on the table. We are waiting."

"Where is Luke?" Joe asked.

"He gorged on mom's cheese and ran himself ragged in the woods playing with the dogs. He crawled into bed and is fast asleep. He can go without supper."

"Rabbit? Where did you get the rabbit?" Pete asked joyously.

Elisa glowed with pleasant revenge, "Women's art--a secret."

"Awh, come on. Where did it come from?"

Rita stubbornly added, "It is a secret."

Andy stroked his beard, looked at Pete and said, "Seems this is a house full of mysteries."